PASS
THE GRAVY

A. A. FAIR

(Erle Stanley Gardner)

PUBLISHED BY POCKET BOOKS NEW YORK

PASS THE GRAVY

William Morrow edition published February, 1961
Pocket Book edition published October, 1962
4th printing . . . February, 1971

This *Pocket Book* edition includes every word
contained in the original, higher-priced edition. It is printed
from brand-new plates made from completely reset, clear, easy-to-read
type. *Pocket Book* editions are published by Pocket Books, a division
of Simon & Schuster, Inc., 630 Fifth Avenue, New York, N.Y. 10020.
Trademarks registered in the United States and other countries.

FOREWORD

THE PROBLEM OF CRIME IS A LOT MORE serious than we realize. Not only does it levy a terrific toll of life and property but it is on the increase and has been on the increase for some time.

Experts who have studied the problem realize that it is unbelievably complex.

The general theory of society is that punishment will put a stop to crime. When a man commits a crime, the police are supposed to catch him, the courts convict him and he is sent to prison for a term of years as punishment. Theoretically, this not only takes the criminal who has committed the crime out of circulation, but the punishment acts as a deterrent to others who might be contemplating the commission of crime.

Unfortunately, a system which works so well in theory functions a lot less efficiently in practice.

For one thing, something like ninety-eight per cent of the persons who are convicted of crime and sent to prison are eventually released to mingle with society. What they do to society after their release depends to a very large extent on what society did to them while they were in prison.

More and more we are coming to realize that each prisoner presents an individual problem. Society has punished him so that the punishment will deter others from committing crime. To that extent punishment is necessary, but punishment can't reform a man, it can only make him bitter. And that brings up the complex problem of what we are going to do with the people who have been sent to prison, during the years of their confinement.

Each prisoner is reduced to a number as far as the prison records are concerned, but each prison inmate was an individual when he went to prison and he remains an individual. There are as many difficult custodial problems as there are types of prisoner and there are almost as many types of prisoner as there are individuals.

To some extent, there are group characteristics which can be counted on. Some prisoners become embittered. Some become melancholy. Some are able to control sexual behavior during the period they are deprived of normal companionship; others are not. Some are underhanded, sneaky opportunists. Some are rugged individuals of the type best described as "outlaw."

No one knows the answers to the highly complex problems of penology but some of the outstanding career penologists in the country have some pretty good ideas as to what should be done and how it should be done.

The trouble is that the individual citizen seldom has any contact with the career penologist. Also, one of the basic problems is that the average citizen has a vindictive streak in his make-up. The criminal has violated the law and has caused society a lot of trouble. The average citizen feels that society should "get even" with the criminal.

This vengeful concept of punishment doesn't work.

For some ten years I have taken an intense interest in prisons and prisoners. The more I see of the problem the more I realize how difficult it is to provide a solution. I don't pretend to know the solution or to try to provide it but I do want to call to the attention of the public some of the outstanding figures in the field of penology.

My friend Robert A. Heinze has been in prison work for some thirty-two years. He started in as chief deputy to the State Parole Officer and was later employed for two years at San Quentin in the capacity of parole officer and placement officer. Then in January of 1944, he became the warden of California's maximum security prison at Folsom. I have known Bob Heinze for years. He is a square shooter, a rugged, two-fisted man who can lay it on the line. When he is dealing with people who want to be tough, Bob Heinze can be tougher than the toughest.

But underneath his tough exterior there is a big heart

and an understanding realization that prisoners are human.

Whenever any inmate wants to meet society halfway, Warden Heinze is there with an encouraging word and a helping hand and when Heinze makes a promise to an inmate he keeps that promise.

It is one of his individual tenets that you can't inculcate a respect for justice in the prison inmate as long as the prison itself is unjust. A prison has to be a place of discipline. At times, the discipline has to be stern and a warden has to be strong enough to make it stern, but the outstanding idea in the back of Bob Heinze's prison philosophy is that a prison should be just.

You can't deal with criminals who have a record as long as your arm in the same way that you would deal with a group of average men, but there are certain basic principles which must be applied if any goodly percentage of those men are to be interested in rehabilitating themselves.

A state can supply all of the rehabilitative facilities in the world and it won't do the least bit of good unless the men themselves are inspired with the idea of rehabilitation.

Statistics show that before this book is out of print a few million citizens will have read it, either in the hard-cover edition or in the paperback edition. I would like those readers to give some thought to the problems of penology and to know something about one of the top men in the field.

And so I dedicate this book to my friend:

ROBERT A. HEINZE,
Warden of the California State Prison at Folsom
(generally referred to as the Folsom State Prison)

Erle Stanley Gardner

CAST OF CHARACTERS

PASS
THE GRAVY

1

THE KID WAS SOMEWHERE AROUND FIFTEEN years old. She was trying her best to be brave and sophisticated.

Bertha Cool was giving her the brush-off.

I stood in the doorway with my hand on the knob and said, "I'm sorry. I didn't know you were busy, Bertha."

"It's all right," Bertha said. "She's leaving."

The kid was blinking to hold back the tears. She didn't want to go, but she wasn't going to beg. She got to her feet with dignity and said, "Thank you very much for giving me your time, Mrs. Cool."

She started toward the door.

I kept standing in the doorway.

Bertha Cool said by way of explanation, "This is my partner, Donald Lam; Sandra Eden, Donald. We have some important business to talk over."

The big blue eyes that were fighting tears tried to smile.

"How do you do, Mr. Lam," she said, with the studied formality of one who was trying her best to be on good behavior.

She moved toward the door but had to stop because I didn't move away from the door.

"Something bothering you, Sandra?" I asked.

She nodded her head, then suddenly tried to push past me.

"It's nothing for us," Bertha said. "There's no money in it—not a dime."

I put my arm around the kid's shoulders. "Hold it, Sandra," I said. "What's the trouble?"

Bertha glared at me. "She's talked to me. I tell you we can't do anything for her."

1

"What is it you want, Sandra?" I asked.

The warmth of my arm around her shoulders and the human sympathy was too much for the kid. She buried her head against my coat and started crying, great convulsive sobs.

"Damn it!" Bertha said, "I hate scenes. Get her out of here."

"We're leaving," I said.

"I want to see *you!*" Bertha yelled.

"See me now, then—while I'm talking with Sandra. Sit down, Sandra."

I piloted her back to the chair.

The kid looked dubiously at Bertha, then sat down on the very edge of the chair.

"What's the trouble?" I asked.

Bertha said, angrily, "There isn't any trouble. Nothing that we can bother about. She wants to locate an Uncle Amos. If Amos is alive, he has some money coming, and if he feels like it he can give Sandra's mother some. Then the mother can pay for some medical expenses and keep the family together. It seems the mother is sick and can't work any more. Even if you locate the uncle, there's no guarantee that he's going to give the mother any money, and if he gives the mother any money, there isn't any fee in it for any detective agency, so for the love of Mike, leave the business end to me and get the kid out of here."

I took Sandra's hand and led her out of Bertha Cool's private office, across the hallway and into my own office.

Elsie Brand, my secretary, looked up and instantly her eyes became sympathetic.

"Come on in and take notes, Elsie," I said.

She seated herself beside Sandra on the davenport, put her arm around the kid's shoulders and said, "What is it?"

Sandra dried her eyes, then smiled, very ladylike, at Elsie and at me and straightened herself. Elsie Brand, with the sort of intuition that good secretaries have, withdrew her arm from around the kid's shoulders.

2

"How did you happen to come in here?" I asked.

"I watch television shows," she said. "I know what a good private detective can do. A librarian friend of mine told me about Cool & Lam, and I always said that if anything ever happened to me I'd go to you folks the very first thing. I asked for you because I'd been told you were the smartest, but you weren't in so Mrs. Cool said she'd see me."

"And what's it all about?" I asked.

"Uncle Amos," she said.

"What's his other name?"

"Gage. Uncle Amos Gage."

"And what about him?"

"Uncle Amos is . . . well, he's peculiar."

I nodded.

"And he goes out on toots . . . neither Mother nor I hold it against him because we don't know enough about alcohol to know about those things. Mother says he's sick. He can't help it when the craving for alcohol hits him, any more than I can help it when I get the measles."

"He's gone now?" I asked.

"He went out on one of his benders and he just never came back. He wrote Mother that he was going to come back, that he'd sobered up and he was hitchhiking home, but he never got there."

"Where's home?" I asked.

"He has his own place but it's not too far from ours—Uncle Amos likes me and he likes Mother."

"Now, he's your mother's brother?" I asked.

"No. Mother was married to *his* brother and then his brother, my father, died and Mother married James Eden and then *they* separated."

"And you still see Uncle Amos?"

"Oh, yes. He's *very* nice. He likes us a lot."

"And what's happened?" I asked.

"Uncle Amos gets money from a trust fund. He gives Mother thirty dollars a month. This month I guess he just didn't get anything—anyhow we haven't seen him."

3

"And you haven't heard from him?"

She shook her head. "Just a post card is all. It said he was on his way back and would see us as soon as he arrived. He never arrived."

"Where does his money come from?" I asked.

"A trust that had been left to him by his uncle."

"Do you know his uncle's name?"

"It was Elbert."

"Do you know how much money?"

She shook her head. "I know it's lots of money but Uncle Amos only gets part of it now. Later on he gets a lot."

"Does your mother know?"

"Of course. He gives Mother thirty dollars a month. He told her that when he got the whole amount of money from the trust fund, he'd give her more. When he's thirty-five he gets it. He told Mother he has made a will leaving her everything in case he should die. I guess Mother and me are the only two people who are really close to him. We like him a lot."

I looked at my watch and said, "I have to see Bertha Cool on a matter of considerable importance. She's waiting for me. You talk to Elsie Brand here and give her your mother's name and your address and if you have a telephone, tell Miss Brand the number. Then you go on home and— You know how to get around the city all right on the buses?"

She gave me an almost withering look. "Of course," she said. "I'm nearly fifteen."

"All right," I told her. "You go on home and then we'll let you know if we find out anything."

"But Mrs. Cool said you couldn't take cases like that, that you would go broke handling kid stuff and . . . and . . ." Her eyes blinked rapidly.

I said, "Bertha Cool has the exterior of a glittering diamond but don't let that fool you. Underneath she has a heart of steel and concrete."

I nodded to Elsie and said, "Get all the dope statistically you can. I'm going into the lion's den."

2

SHAPE, WEIGHT AND HATE. BERTHA COOL always reminded me of a big spool of barbed wire.

Now she glared at me with bitter animosity in her little glittering eyes. "Prince Charming," she said. "Santa Claus! So you've made me the mean old witch so you could play Prince Charming to the brat."

"I thought I'd find out what it was she wanted," I said.

"I know what she wants," Bertha Cool said. "She wants sympathy, affection and charity. That's the worst of you. You have all the obnoxious qualities of the fatuous male sex. Let a woman of any age bat her eyes at you and squeeze out a tear and you're patting her on the shoulder and trying to find out what you can do for her.

"If you weren't such a damn fool you'd realize the facts of life. That brat has a mother. The mother is old enough to have sense. When she sends that kid around to a detective agency, it's because she's trying to pull a sympathy racket, not because the mother doesn't feel well enough to come."

I just stood there and smiled. "What was it you wanted to see me about?" I asked.

"I don't know as I ever want to see you again," Bertha said. "You and your grand manners! You and your big-hearted sympathy! You and your soft-touch personality! Honest to God, Donald, if I didn't sit on the lid here you'd give this whole goddam detective agency away in the first thirty days."

"Will it keep?" I asked.

"Will *what* keep?"

"What you wanted to see me about."

"Hell no, it won't keep."

"In that case you'd better tell me," I said.

"Oh no," Bertha said sarcastically, "it isn't important.

Just a retainer of five hundred bucks, fifty dollars a day for an operative, three hundred for expenses, and a five-hundred-dollar bonus if we get the thing definitely solved either one way or the other within a week."

The diamonds on Bertha's fingers made a glittering semi-circle as she moved her hands in a quick gesture of throwing something into the wastebasket. "But *we* don't want it. Oh no, not us! We're too proud and independent to worry about money. Let the office expenses take care of themselves. Throw the cash away while we go chasing mirages. The firm of Cool & Lam is working for a bunch of kids!"

Bertha warmed up to her subject. She pretended to pick up the telephone. "What's that . . . ? Two thousand dollars . . . ? I'm sorry, we're not interested. The full facilities of the firm are engaged in locating a missing choo-choo car for a five-year-old who can't remember where she put it."

Bertha pretended to slam up the telephone.

I opened the door.

"Where the hell are *you* going?" Bertha screamed at me.

"Out," I said. "I've got work to do."

"Work for a flat-chested, spindle-shanked brat with blue eyes! Damn it! Come back here and listen to sense."

"I haven't heard any so far."

Bertha clenched her bulldog jaw. Her jowls quivered with indignation. She flashed diamonds once more as her hands moved in picking up some notes. "Get this," she said. "Malcolm Greenlease Beckley disappeared over a week ago. His wife, Daphne Beckley, is frantic. She wants to find the guy."

"Why?" I asked.

"Why?" Bertha Cool was screaming again. "How the hell do I know? I suppose it's because she loves the sonofabitch!"

"Any insurance angle?"

"What made you ask that?"

"Because of the five-hundred-dollar bonus," I said.

"Women don't usually get bonus-minded after only a week of separation."

Bertha's eyes tried to show animosity but showed interest instead. "You're a brainy little bastard, Donald," she said with grudging admiration. "Sometimes I wonder how you do it—and other times I wonder how you lived this long without having designing women pick the gold fillings out of your teeth, steal the shirt off your back and toss you to the fishes."

"Then there is insurance?"

"Seventy-five G's," Bertha said, "and double indemnity in case of accidental death."

"So where do we begin?" I asked.

"*You* begin," she said, "by talking with Mrs. Beckley. Her first name is Daphne. She sounds like a dish."

"And you're letting *me* talk with her?" I asked.

"Don't worry," she said. "All the financial details have been arranged. You can go on out there and let her cross her legs and pull all the cheesecake she wants. It won't do a damned bit of good. The fee's fixed—and just to tell you something about her type of woman, Donald, she won't even bat an eyelash at you now. She knows she can't get even a five-cent discount out of me and knowing that, you'll find that your anxious little client is sitting there very demurely—but if big Bertha hadn't fixed the fee, you'd have found her making goo-goo eyes at you and crossing her legs until you'd have had to wear dark glasses to keep your eyes from being put out by the nylon."

"Where do I find her?" I asked.

"The Ringold Apartments. She's in 721 and she's expecting you. You get over there and she'll tell you the whole story; that is, unless she's changed her mind on account of all the delay while you were playing Uncle Dudley to that gangling brat."

"What about the expenses?" I asked Bertha.

"We got three hundred bucks for expenses," Bertha said, "and if the expenses run any more than that, we pay for them out of our fee."

7

"That's not enough," I told her.

"It will have to be enough."

"All right," I said, "I'll make a check for three hundred dollars on the expense account."

Bertha glowered at me and said, "You *could* start out with fifty dollars and then come and get more if you had to."

"That's not my way of working," I said. "I start out with three hundred and then if there's any left I put it back."

Bertha's face started to color. She sucked in her breath as a prelude to some outburst of indignation, but I didn't wait for it to mature. I stepped out, pulled the door closed, and walked back to my office.

Sandra Eden was still talking with Elsie Brand.

"Any pictures?" I asked Elsie, glancing at the information she'd jotted down.

"She thinks her mother has one."

"How did you come?" I asked Sandra.

"By bus."

"Want to go home by car?"

"With you?"

I nodded.

Her eyes lit up. "I'd love it," she said.

"Come on," I told her.

Elsie Brand watched us with speculative eyes as we left the office.

I had the cashier give me three hundred bucks on an expense voucher, seated Sandra Eden in the agency heap and we drove out to see her mother.

It was a rather shoddy apartment house, and Mrs. Eden obviously hadn't expected visitors.

"I'm a fright," she said. "I can't talk with you now."

"What do you want to do?" I asked.

"Well . . . put on something respectable."

"It's your voice I'm interested in," I told her. "You can't dress up your voice. Anyway, I'm crowded for time."

She tried to be exasperated but there was too much affection in her eyes and voice as she looked at Sandra.

8

"Sandra told me she was going to see you people. I told her she couldn't possibly interest a detective agency. It takes money to run an investigation."

"It does for a fact," I said.

"Well," she said with a forced laugh, "that's one of the things that we're fresh out of."

"You've been working?" I asked.

"*Have* been," she said.

"Gave it up on account of ill health?"

"They gave me up—they let me go because they thought I was too slow. I . . . I would work there when I was almost ready to double up with pain, but I'd keep fighting it and—"

"What's the matter?" I asked.

She said, "I think I have . . . a tumor. The doctors wanted to operate six months ago."

"And you haven't been back for six months?"

"I've had to work. I can't afford an operation just at present."

I got up, walked out to the kitchenette and opened the ice box. There was a carton of milk and not very much else. No butter, no eggs, no meat.

She was angry. "What are you doing walking out into my kitchen and making yourself at home?"

"Just checking," I said.

"Well, Mr. Lam, I'll thank you to . . ." Her voice broke. "All right, I can't afford to be proud," she said.

"What about Uncle Amos?"

"His name is Amos Gage. There's money coming to him from a trust fund left him by an uncle."

"What was the uncle's name?"

"Elbert."

"And what about the money?"

"It's in trust. If Amos Gage is alive at the age of thirty-five and has not been convicted of any crime, the money goes to him outright. If he dies before reaching the age of thirty-five or if he has been convicted of crime, the money goes to various charitable institutions."

"How old is he now?"

9

"He'll be thirty-five in a couple of weeks. In the meantime the trustee gives him a small income."

"That's a tricky situation," I said. "Driving while intoxicated would bring him right under the gun."

"Why do you say that?"

"Say what?"

"Driving while intoxicated."

"Because it's a crime. Lots of people commit that crime to a greater or lesser degree."

"Well, that's . . . that's . . . I think, what bothered his uncle. You see, Uncle Amos is a periodic drinker."

I nodded.

"Did Sandra tell you?"

"I'm just checking on the facts," I said. "We can save a lot of time if you'll do the talking."

"You—I mean, is your agency going to work on it?"

"I don't know yet. I hope we can work something out."

"I don't have any money."

"I know."

"And if you find him, it may be the worst thing that could happen."

"How come?"

"I'm afraid he's been driving while intoxicated and is locked up somewhere. He'd have been smart enough to give an assumed name."

"How about his driving license?"

"He wouldn't have made the mistake of producing that. He'd have ditched it somewhere."

"He's smart?" I asked.

"He's pretty smart," she said. "About some things."

"All right," I said, "we find him and if he's in jail for drunk driving, then what?"

"He loses the money."

"How much money?"

"I understand it's become seven hundred and fifty thousand now. It was around half a million but it's been invested in securities, and the securities have been going up."

I said, "Suppose we find him and he isn't in jail. Then what?"

10

"Then he'd help me. I need his help particularly this month, but I'm afraid he— That's all I can think of, Mr. Lam. I'm terribly afraid that's why no one has heard from him. I'm afraid he's in jail somewhere."

"All right," I said, "suppose he's in jail and is trying to cover up so that the trustee doesn't find out about it. Then we find him. That's jerking the rug right out from under you and Uncle Amos."

She nodded.

"It would give a detective agency a swell opportunity for blackmail."

"I didn't know they did that in real life."

"Neither did I. I was just refreshing your memory from the books, the movies and television."

She smiled, a rather faint, wan smile.

I looked her over. She had a waxy complexion. She hadn't bothered to put on any war paint or lipstick. She was wearing a housecoat, and the blue eyes had a sunken, tired look.

"You said you'd been to a doctor."

"Yes."

"Who is he?"

"Dr. Mortinsen L. Beach. He's a famous specialist in . . . women's diseases."

"And he wanted to operate?"

"Yes."

"What makes you think this Uncle Amos, as you call him, would let you have money if he had it?"

"He's very generous. He's a real friend. He was my first husband's brother. He's been giving me thirty dollars a month to help out—that was before I lost my job. Now I'm desperate."

"When did you last hear from him?"

She said, "I'm going to trust you, Mr. Lam."

"It always helps," I told her, "particularly if you want results."

"Uncle Amos is a periodic drunkard. He goes on these binges and, because he knows what's going to happen if he's caught driving a car while intoxicated, whenever he

11

takes the first drink he puts the key to his car in an envelope and sends it to me."

"He lives near here?"

"Next door."

"Apartment?"

"No, that bungalow."

"Where does he keep the car?"

"In the garage in the back."

"All right, he sends you the key. Then what?"

"Then I hold the key until he's completely over his binge. Sometimes he'll show up and beg for the car key, but I won't give it to him unless I know he's over it."

"How do you tell when he's over it?"

"Well, there's a difference. It's hard to tell you in words."

"You were married to his brother?"

"That's right."

"The brother died?"

"Yes."

"And you married again?"

"Yes."

"Sandra was the child of the first marriage?"

"Yes. She changed her name when I married James Eden."

"Why?"

"The family always hated me—all except Amos."

"How about Elbert?"

"He never acknowledged me. After my first husband died, Elbert never even spoke to me—or to Sandra."

"What was your first husband's name?"

"Norman Gage."

I let it go at that.

Mrs. Eden waited for a moment, then went on. "Getting back to Amos," she said, "this time I got an envelope with the key to the car. I knew that Uncle Amos was out somewhere, probably getting ready for a premature celebration of his thirty-fifth birthday. I was terribly worried and apprehensive."

"And then what?"

12

"Several days ago I got a post card. It had been sent from Carver City. It said he had sobered up and was coming home."

"From Carver City?"

"Yes."

"How was he planning to get home if you have his car key and if he's broke?"

"He hitchhikes."

I raised my eyebrows.

"When Uncle Amos goes on a bender," she said, "he —I want you to understand, Mr. Lam, it's some sort of a strange compulsion. It isn't that he just wants to drink, it's some definite psychological or physiological craving. It—"

"You can waste a lot of time trying to explain the periodic drunkard," I said. "Nobody understands him."

"Well, that's the way it is with Uncle Amos. Anyway, he drinks until his money is gone. He gets an income from the trust fund of three hundred dollars a month. It's what they call a spendthrift trust, I believe. His uncle didn't want him to be trusted with much more than enough money to live on."

I nodded.

"Then when he goes broke, he usually goes to a service station that's run by an Elk."

"Why an Elk?"

"Because he's a member of the Order of Elks. He says he can always find a service station man who's an Elk. He meets this man, tells him who he is and what he's up against and asks the man to help him catch a ride."

"The service station man will?"

"Sometimes he actually helps him get a ride. Sometimes the service station man will just pretend he doesn't notice that Uncle Amos is hanging around the service station. Then Uncle Amos will wait until some man comes along who looks like a likely customer, preferably some Elk."

"And then Uncle Amos gets home?"

"He gets home. Sometimes he does it in three or four installments. Sometimes he gets a car that is coming right on through."

13

"And this time you got a card from Uncle Amos?"

"Sent from Carver City. It said everything was okay, that he had weathered the worst of the storm and was all right, that he was flat broke, that he was waiting out there at a service station that was run by an Elk. He said we could expect him within twenty-four hours."

"And then what?"

"Absolute silence," she said.

"You thought of notifying the police?" I asked.

"I thought of it and I'm afraid to."

"Why?"

"Because if the police find out anything there it would be official."

"Well?"

"If he was in jail, they'd make a note of it and report it."

"And as far as we're concerned . . . ?"

"A private agency could find him and . . . well, if I were your client you could protect me, couldn't you? You wouldn't have to tell everybody *all* you knew. You could perhaps help get him out of jail so that . . . well, so it wouldn't be publicized."

"You mean you'd cheat the trust by concealing information from the trustee?"

She lowered her eyes for a moment, then raised them and looked defiantly into mine. "Yes," she said. "It was a cruel, unjust provision in the will. It did a lot to rob Uncle Amos of his self-confidence. If they'd just let Uncle Amos alone, he'd have worked it out all right. He realizes he needs treatment, but that trustee is a self-righteous, pompous individual who is completely patronizing, sadistic and egotistic.

"Under the terms of the trust, Uncle Amos gets three hundred a month but in order to get it he has to appear personally at the office of the trustee. The trustee gives him the three hundred dollars in cash, and Uncle Amos signs a receipt. Every time, the trustee gives Uncle Amos a lecture about straightening up, about making something out of himself. Uncle Amos gets so mad, he goes out and

14

sputters around; sometimes it's the trigger that releases this appetite that is hidden in Uncle Amos' disposition and he starts drinking."

I looked at Sandra. "Sandra knows all about this, I take it."

"Sandra has my complete confidence," Mrs. Eden said, "and I have hers."

"Got a picture?" I asked.

"I have a snapshot that was taken about six months ago of the three of us together."

"A good likeness?"

"I think it is—of course it's a snapshot, not a portrait, but I think it's a pretty good likeness."

"Let's take a look. I'd like to see the post card, too, if you have it."

She walked over to a shelf of books, picked out a volume of *The Adventures of Ellery Queen.* Next to it was a three-volume set of Sherlock Holmes, *Ride the Pink Horse,* by Dorothy Hughes, stories of Nero Wolfe by Rex Stout, and a volume entitled *The Murders of Los Angeles.*

I raised my eyebrows.

"Sandra's," she explained. "The child simply devours mysteries and true murder stories. Here's the picture. I keep it in a book so it won't curl up."

"I'm training my powers of reasoning that way," Sandra explained. "And now we have a real honest-to-goodness detective right here in the house, Mother."

"I'm afraid you were too impulsive, dear," the mother said with a tolerant, forgiving smile.

She handed me the picture, then went over to a table, picked up a post card and gave it to me. I looked them over, put the photo in my pocket and said, "You haven't heard anything from Amos Gage since Carver City?"

"That's the last I've heard."

"Okay," I said, handing her the card, "I'll toss it around a bit and let you know whether we can handle it."

I shook hands with her, and Sandra, acting the perfect little hostess, escorted me to the door.

I went down the stairs. There was a combined delicatessen and grocery store across the street. I took twenty-five dollars of the partnership expense account and handed it to the manager of the store.

"What's this for?"

I said, "Do you know a little girl named Sandra Eden from the apartment across the street? She has—"

"Yes, yes, I know her. They buy food here sometimes. I haven't seen her for a few days."

"Know her mother?"

"I've seen her mother. I don't know her as well as the girl."

I said, "You know the sort of groceries they generally buy?"

He nodded.

"All right," I said, "fix up a basket with some of those groceries in it. Put in a couple of good steaks and a chicken. Go over to Apartment 305, which is where they live, knock at the door and deliver the basket. They'll ask you where it came from. Tell them that a perfect stranger came in and said Uncle Amos wanted them to have some groceries."

"Who?"

"Uncle Amos."

"Uncle Amos," he said, "why, that's Amos Gage! He lives over there in that—"

"You're talking," I said, "when you should be listening. A *representative* of Uncle Amos wanted them to have this."

"A *representative* of Uncle Amos," he echoed.

"Now you've got it," I told him, "and if they ask you what he looked like you don't remember. Get that stuff up there right away. Got it?"

"I've got it," he said.

"All right," I told him, "get on the ball."

I went down the street to a telephone booth and looked up Dr. Mortinsen L. Beach.

I rang the office, a secretary answered, I said I wanted to talk with Dr. Beach, that it was a matter of some importance and was advised that it was impossible.

I asked if I could talk with his nurse and was told *that* was impossible. I told them it was about making arrangements for an operation on one of his patients. Then the nurse came to the telephone.

I said, "This is a representative of Amos Gage. I understand you have a patient, an Eleanore Eden, who has been advised to have an operation. I'd like to know about what it's going to cost."

"Who is this?" she asked.

"A representative of Amos Gage. She's a relative," I said.

She said, "Just a minute."

After a little while a man's voice came on the telephone, a crisp, professional but deeply sympathetic voice. "This is Dr. Beach," he said. "I'd like to find out definitely with whom I'm talking."

"A representative of Amos Gage," I said, "who is a relative of Eleanore Eden. She needs an operation and I'd like to know how serious it is, and how much it's going to cost."

"She's badly in need of an operation," Dr. Beach said. "I don't discuss a patient's condition with any other person, even a relative, unless I am specifically instructed to do so. But I can tell you that there is a condition there which should be cleared up by an operation. I have every reason to believe that it is not too late at the present time, but I also have every reason to believe that if the condition is permitted to continue, there will be an involvement of surrounding tissue. At any time now the situation may become more than we can cope with. Now, will you please come to my office and tell me who you are and—"

"How much is the operation going to cost, Doctor?" I asked.

"Cost!" he snapped into the telephone, "Cost, hell! Let's get the operation done. We'll talk about the cost and how I can get paid afterwards, but the main thing is she's got to have one hundred and fifty dollars when she enters the hospital. I can donate my time on credit but I can't go around putting up hospital fees. She told me she

17

had a relative who might advance her the money but that it would be a few months before he had sufficient money. I trust I'm not being indiscreet, but that woman needs an operation. I can cure her if I can get my hands on her but I can't pay her hospital bills."

"Your fee can wait?"

"My fee can wait or can be thrown out of the window," the doctor snapped. "Now will you get up here?"

"I'll be up," I said and then added, "but I don't know just when," and hung up before he could do anything about it.

3

I CALLED THE *Daily Tribune* AND ASKED for the reference library.

As soon as Marlene Hyde, who had charge of the newspaper morgue, came on the phone, I said, "Hello, beautiful, this is Donald."

"Donald!" she exclaimed. *"Where* have you been keeping yourself?"

"Busy."

"I don't *ever* see you any more."

"I'm chasing murderers to their lair," I explained.

"Well, you'd better get up here to do some research work and let your head save your heels."

"Now *there's* an idea!" I said. "How about getting some stuff all lined up so I run in and out?"

"Can do," she said, "but you don't *always* need to be in such a hurry."

"You speed up my metabolism," I told her. "I always get hungry and have to go eat."

"Why didn't you tell me? I'll bake a pie and bring it to the office."

"It's a deal," I said. "In the meantime, look up a fellow

18

by the name of Elbert Gage who died several years ago and left a fortune in trust for a nephew named Amos. There's some sort of a spendthrift trust connected with it. The paper probably carried a story on it at the time."

"What's the name? Gage?"

"That's right."

"G-a-g-e?"

"Right."

"I'll have it for you. When will you be up?"

"Fifteen minutes."

"I'll be watching the door."

"No fooling?"

"No fooling," and then she added hurriedly, "at least not on my part," and hung up the telephone before I could say anything.

I piloted the agency heap up to a parking place near the *Tribune*.

Marlene had red hair and the complexion that went with it. She also had a pert turned-up nose and a figure which had been good enough to get her elected a Miss Something-or-other three or four years ago. There had been a lot of newspaper publicity about her. One time, just to annoy her, I asked for the *Tribune* file on Hyde, and before she knew what I was looking for, had pulled out all of the clippings showing the Marlene Hyde cheesecake at the time she was Miss Voltage at the Electricians' Convention, or whatever it was.

"I'm surprised you still know your way up here," Marlene said.

"Has it been that long?"

"It's been that long." She slipped her hand on the inside of my arm, led me over to a table and said, "What have you been doing, and what about that perfectly horrible partner of yours?"

"She's not perfectly horrible," I said. "She makes horrible noises, that's all."

"She's detestable. You know something, Donald?"

"What?"

"She's terribly afraid that you're going to get married,

19

that that will bring another feminine mind into the business and . . . oh, it's hard to explain. Bertha loves you, in a way."

"And in a way," I said, "she hates my guts."

Marlene nodded. "It's a strange combination. I don't think your Bertha Cool likes men."

"She had a marriage go sour on her years ago," I said.

"That's *her* story," Marlene said. "I'll bet she went sour on marriage."

"Anyway, she's sour."

"That's for sure."

"Anything else you want to talk about?" I asked.

"Any suggestions?"

"How did we happen to start talking about marriage?"

"I brought it up," she said. "I thought I'd done it subtly."

"You did. I was just wondering how it happened."

"Men always do. They're led into the subject when what they have in mind is something altogether different."

"Such as what?"

"Now who's leading whom? Come on, Donald, get into your act. It's time for you to tell me what a big hurry you're in and that you have to have the Gage file."

"I'm in a hurry," I said, "and have to have the Gage file."

She brought out an envelope and I went through it.

There was a picture of the decedent and a picture of Amos. It was a picture that had been taken ten years before. Uncle Amos looked like the flaming youth of the period.

There was a copy of the provision in the will to the effect that the testator, having much love and affection for his brother's son, being entirely without relatives of his own but doubting the ability of his nephew to comport himself in a proper and fitting manner in the event he should suddenly inherit a large sum of money, was leaving the entire estate in trust for the following purposes, to wit:

I skimmed through the powers that were given the trustees. It was one of those spendthrift trusts which vested discretion in the trustee as to the amount which was to be given the beneficiary up to the age of thirty-five. At the age of thirty-five, if Amos Gage had not died and had not been convicted of any major crime during that period, the money was to go absolutely to Amos Gage and the trust was to be terminated.

Otherwise, in the event the said Amos Gage had died prior to attaining the age of thirty-five or had been convicted of any major crime, then and in that event, one half of the money was to go to the following institutions in which the testator had an interest and with whose objectives he found himself in complete accord, the balance was to go to any heirs who could be found other than Amos Gage or any descendant of his. Then followed a list of the institutions which included various and sundry educational and charitable institutions.

The trustee in whom the testator expressed unlimited confidence was Jerome L. Campbell. In the event he should die before the trust had expired, his place was to be taken by an alternate who was named, and in the event of the alternate's death another alternate was named. I gathered from the clippings that Campbell was a banker and the two alternate trustees were lawyers.

I went back to Marlene's desk and found her answering the telephone. Some reporter was evidently handing her a great line. She was laughing and tracing little designs on the counter with the tip of her forefinger while she talked.

I sneaked up behind her, put my finger on the telephone and broke the connection.

She whirled angrily. Her face was within inches of mine, her eyes were blazing and then suddenly the blaze went out of them and she was tilting her face.

I kissed her.

It was the second time in my life I had kissed her. That kiss was all anyone could expect from a redhead.

When she broke away her face was flushed.

"I'd love to think you sneaked up behind me just to do that," she said, "but instinct tells me you only want another

21

clipping and couldn't wait for the phone conversation to terminate naturally."

"Jerome L. Campbell," I said.

She looked at me appraisingly. "A gentleman would at least have lied about it."

"All right," I said, "let's try it over again."

She gave me a token slap, flounced away into the filing room and came back with Jerome L. Campbell's file.

There wasn't anything really worth saving in the lot. The things had just been clipped out to give a background on a man whose name was more or less prominent in financial circles.

Campbell had addressed the banking convention. Campbell had made the address of welcome at the Better Business Bureau convention. Campbell had been one of the judges at the intercollege debate.

Phooey on that stuff! I got the guy's address and handed the envelope back to Marlene.

Some reporter was in a hurry for information, and Marlene had to be dancing attendance on him. I could see that she wanted to break away to tell me something before I left, but the reporter was demanding lots of service.

I went down to the office of Jerome Campbell and told his secretary I wanted to see him about the Gage estate.

There was a bit of telephoning, and then I was permitted to go in.

Campbell was a big man with cold, candid eyes. He had practiced an expression of wide-eyed sincerity until it had frozen on his face. When he talked, he had a habit of spreading both hands apart as though ridding himself of every vestige of subterfuge.

He was big-framed and he'd begun to put on fat.

He sized me up with the patronizing attitude which so many big men feel for a guy who is only five-foot-six and weighs a hundred and thirty-five.

"Mister Lam," he said, as though he had been pronouncing the name of a dog that had been brought up in a dog show.

I said, "What about the trust in the Gage estate?"

"What's your interest in it?"

"I want a story."

"Newspaper reporter?" he asked.

"Let's say I'm free-lancing," I said. "I just came from the *Tribune*. I've been looking the situation up in their morgue, getting all the information on it."

"I feel certain you don't need any more from me then."

"I do. According to the records, Amos Gage is to become thirty-five on the twenty-fifth of this month. What's happened to the trust?"

"Nothing has happened to the trust," Campbell said coldly.

"You haven't prepared to turn it over?"

"Why should I? The conditions have not as yet been fulfilled."

"What conditions?"

"The conditions of the trust. For all I know, Amos Gage may be in jail someplace."

"And you wouldn't pay over the money if he should be in jail?"

"You've read the provisions of the trust," he said.

I nodded.

"If he's in jail the entire fund would go to various charities."

"I may say, Mr. Lam, that if you want to write this situation up, I would certainly appreciate having it written from the angle of the devastating effect of alcohol on a man's character. I am violating no confidence in telling you that Amos Gage is a heavy drinker. His uncle knew that and deprecated the fact."

I said, "You give Amos a monthly allowance?"

"A monthly allowance, the amount of which was left almost entirely to my discretion. Under the will, I had to give him a minimum of three hundred dollars a month. More I could give him at my discretion."

"What happens to the three hundred a month once he's past thirty-five?"

"That, of course, is terminated. The entire trust will

23

have terminated one way or another at that time. However, if the funds go to the various charities, I am to remain as trustee for an additional period of three years to liquidate the assets into cash. I may say that the will was hurriedly drawn, but it is legal. Elbert Gage put off drawing the will until the last minute. He died less than thirty days after executing the will. It was a tragic situation—a man having no living relative to whom he dared bequeath a fortune. It is a terrible indictment of the devastating effect of acohol on a man's character."

"I gather," I said, "that if the property should go to Amos, it will be turned over in the form of the various income-producing securities when he becomes thirty-five?"

"That is right, but only if it goes to Amos. If it is to go to the charities named, I am to remain in office for three years, gradually liquidating the securities so they will, in my judgment, produce the greatest sum of cash."

"You get paid for your services?"

"I draw compensation."

"How much?"

"None of your business."

"How do you pay Gage the monthly allowance? Send him a check?" I asked.

"I certainly do not. I regard my responsibilities under the trust far too seriously to dispose of them in such a casual manner. I have Mr. Gage come to my office personally every time a monthly installment is to be paid over. I pay in the form of cash and take his receipt."

"How many months have you given him *more* than the three hundred dollars?"

"I have *never* given him more than the three hundred dollars," Campbell said. "He never showed a sufficient desire to reform to warrant an increase in his allowance."

"Are you," I asked, "going to take it on yourself to find Amos Gage when the trust terminates and ascertain whether he is—"

"I certainly am not," Campbell said. "I am trustee. It is up to Mr. Gage to come to me on his thirty-fifth birthday and convince me that the conditions of the trust have been fulfilled. Due to the fact that the time for his last allowance has passed and he has not put in an appearance, I may state, Mr. Lam, that there is an increasing suspicion on my part that all is not well."

"What do you mean, all is not well?"

"I think perhaps he is in trouble, perhaps in jail. I feel he is being restrained against his will."

"And if he is?"

"If he is in jail, the money goes to various charitable enterprises."

"I take it," I said, "you're checking every step with your lawyers."

His face reddened. "What do you mean, lawyers? I have no use for lawyers. I go into court every year with my accounts. I appear on my own behalf. Last year the court complimented me on the meticulous care with which the account had been prepared."

"If you're acting as your own lawyer," I said, "you'd better take another good long look at the trust."

"What do you mean?"

"Under the terms of the trust," I said, "you pay over the money if he's still alive and hasn't been convicted of a major crime by the time he's thirty-five."

"That's right. There's no question about that."

"What about the word 'major'?" I asked.

"Any crime is a *major* crime," he said unctuously. "Anything which could possibly have resulted in a jail sentence would be a major crime. I know how the testator felt. I feel the same way."

"There's one other word you may not have thought about," I said.

"What's that word?"

"Convicted."

Campbell started to say something, then suddenly changed his mind. He paused, took a long breath. "You mean that . . ." He stopped in mid-sentence and started thinking the situation over.

"Exactly," I said. "I mean that even if Amos Gage has

25

been apprehended in the act of committing a murder, has been arrested for murder and has been tried for murder, but if the jury doesn't bring in its verdict *prior* to the twenty-fifth of this month, you're going to have to pay over the trust fund."

"Why," he said, "that's ... that's ridiculous, Mr. Lam!"

"Those are the terms of the trust."

"Well, that's not the spirit of the trust."

"What controls a trust of that sort?" I asked innocently. "The words or the spirit?"

"I—Mr. Lam, are you deliberately trying to bait me?"

"Not me," I told him. "You've already taken the hook without the necessity of anyone having to use any bait."

I walked out, leaving him glaring at me.

4

So THAT BERTHA WOULDN'T BE SCREAMING her head off in case Mrs. Beckley called again and mentioned that I hadn't been there, I put off a couple of other things I wanted to do, drove to the Ringold Apartments and went up to 721.

Daphne Beckley was a striking brunette. Her hair was midnight black with glossy highlights. Her eyes were black pools. Her figure was slender at the waist but full of curves. She was under thirty. She might have been no more than twenty-five. The only thing wrong with her was her mouth. The lips were too thick, but she was clever with make-up, and from a distance her mouth was rose-budded into an attractive shape that looked a bit too large.

She knew all about her curves and all about how to display them to advantage.

Some women can strut their stuff and it's just a wiggle; others can twist a hip and it's a soft, undulating, come-hither gesture that is almost a caress. You can't tell for

26

certain just what makes the difference, but the strip-teasers have it, some more than others.

A good strip-teaser can take off her gloves and make it seem positively naughty. That was Daphne Beckley. She looked at me, averted her eyes, looked at me again and said throatily, "Oh, yes, Mr. Lam. Your partner said you'd be here."

Her voice and the gesture made it seem that we were having a bedroom rendezvous, despite the fact that she decorously seated herself in a chair after I had moved over to stand by the davenport.

I tried to be breezily businesslike. "I understand," I said, opening a notebook for no particular reason except that it was a good prop, "your husband has disappeared and you want him back."

The long-lidded black eyes flashed a glance at me, then were suddenly lowered as though she wanted to keep me from reading her particular thoughts. "It may be," she said in a low voice, "that I won't want him back. At this time I only want to know what became of him. My sentiments are frankly more mercenary than connubial."

"I see," I said.

"You don't see at all," she charged. "You're just saying that to be nice. Actually, I've shocked you. You're not accustomed to having women be that frank, are you?"

"I can never get accustomed to women," I said. "They're full of surprises."

"Well," she said coyly, "I'm unusual in that I'm frank. I can afford to be frank. I've never found it necessary to resort to subterfuge. If I like someone, I say so. If I don't like people, they find it out."

"And what is your present state of mind as far as your husband is concerned?"

"Now that," she said, crossing her knees and running the tips of the fingers of her right hand over the knee of her stocking, "is something that I don't know myself.

"Perhaps in justice to myself, Mr. Lam, I should tell you that when last seen on the night of the fifth, my

27

husband was traveling with a blond hitchhiker. He had been faithfully telephoning me every night until this buxom female tramp entered the picture. After that he seems to have gone off the deep end."

"It would help," I said, "if I knew the facts."

"My husband is a salesman," she said. "He's rather a good salesman, but very frankly, Mr. Lam, we don't save very much money. If I should file for a divorce, there wouldn't be enough property to divide up to pay the court costs. On the other hand, my husband has a large income—which he spends—and I've always been able to help him."

I nodded and kept my notebook open, taking out a fountain pen from my pocket and holding the point poised an inch and a half above the page. Experience has taught me that with a certain type of client this air of expectation produces results.

She said, "If I'm going to divorce him, I want alimony. I'm not going to mince words with you, Mr. Lam. If I can catch him stepping out, I want to catch him right in the act. I want to catch him so hard and so fast that there's no question about it."

"I'm afraid you've come to the wrong agency. We don't do divorce work."

"This isn't divorce work," she said. "This is investigative work. There's a difference. I explained it to Mrs. Cool over the telephone and she agreed to accept my case. She said she was the business head of your firm, and I consider that matter as settled.

"Also, I don't think my husband has simply gone philandering. I think something else has happened. My husband would not have remained away all this time without getting in touch with me. Even if this blonde is good, she's not *that* good.

"You see, my husband is ten years older than I am. To put the matter upon a chart of biological probabilities, Malcolm would never have noticed a woman unless she had a very high voltage.

"Malcolm has always been glad to get home and very,

very glad to get home when he's been away for a week at a time. This time he's been gone ten days."

I said, "That might mean he was in a mood when all women looked unusually attractive to him."

"Let's concede that, Mr. Lam. We're not children. We may as well face facts. But he was hurrying home. He was impatient to get here. He had dropped me a post card from Carver City and had phoned me at the same time. Then he telephoned me again from Central Creek. And then, because he had a flat tire, he had his blonde hitchhiker call me from Rommelly."

"All on the fifth?"

"All on the fifth," she said. "Although technically the blonde's call was the morning of the sixth.

"You see, my husband called me from Carver City. At that time he thought he was going to have to drive to Reno to see a man there the next day. He also sent me a post card from Carver City. That's when he told me he'd be driving most of the night and said there was a hitchhiker there he was going to pick up to spell him on the driving."

"I see. How far is Carver City from here?"

"About two hundred and forty miles. He told me there were lots of fishermen on the road, driving—as he expressed it—like a bat out of hell."

"Naturally he was trying to keep out of the way of those oncoming cars," I said.

"Naturally."

"Do you have the post card?"

"Certainly."

"A picture of him?"

"Of course. I wouldn't have called in a detective agency otherwise. I know you're skilled workers in the investigative field, but even so, you can't simply pull a rabbit out of the hat."

"May I see the post card?"

"Of course," she said. "I have it here for you. This is the one from Carver City."

I thought back to the post card sent from Carver City by Uncle Amos.

"Did your husband usually send post cards?" I asked.

"Very seldom," she said. "He doesn't like people to read his business mail and when he's away from home he prefers to use a more private means of communication than the post card."

"He phoned you from Carver City?"

"And later on from Central Creek."

"I see. Then the post card was from Carver City?"

"Yes."

"Why would he phone you and then send you a post card?"

"He sent me the post card telling me a few sweet nothings, then phoned me, and then twenty miles farther on he decided to phone me again."

"When he sent the post card, he must have known he would see you before the card reached you."

"No, he didn't. When he mailed the card and when he phoned me the first time, he thought he was going to have to go to Reno to keep a date with a customer there. But after he had mailed the card and phoned me from Carver City, he phoned the customer just to check on the appointment and learned the customer was sick.

"So then he decided to drive on home and that's why he phoned from Central Creek."

"But you said he didn't ordinarily use post cards?"

"That's right."

"What caused him to make an exception this time?"

"Just being devilish, I guess," she said, and laughed. "When he talked with me on the phone he told me about the post card. He said that this service station at Carver City was trying a new publicity stunt. It furnished stamped post cards all ready for mailing. The cards were free. Anybody could send them free—of course the joker was that the cards had a picture of the service station and some advertising matter on the front."

"I see," I said. "Let's take a look."

She handed me a glazed picture post card.

The picture was of a pretty good-looking service station that had a sign over it, CARLYLE KAMP SERVICE. On the opposite side was printed, in small type, "Carlyle Kamp's Service Station at Carver City is at the entrance to some of the best fishing and hunting territory in the state. Carlyle Kamp makes it a point to keep in touch with varying conditions throughout this territory so that he can give up-to-the-minute information to sportsmen. Kamp's Service Station has spacious, spotlessly clean rest rooms, telephone booths which open out from an air-conditioned office, a drinking fountain with crystal-clear ice water, and vending machines for cigarettes and various cold drinks. Make it a point to stop in at Carlyle Kamp, the friendly service station."

This side of the post card had the right-hand side reserved for the address, and on the left side, beneath the paragraph of ballyhoo, was room for a brief message.

Malcolm Beckley had scribbled in the message space, "Am going to Reno, sweetheart, but will be pulsing for you every minute and every mile. A hitchhiker here looks like a good guy. I'm going to take a chance on him."

The post card was signed simply, "Malcolm G. B."

"G?" I asked.

"Greenlease. G-r-double e-n-l-e-a-s-e," she said.

"And the B is Beckley?"

She nodded.

"Now then, he also called you up from Central Creek?"

"Yes. That was half an hour later, around midnight. He sounded just like his usual, normal self, only he was jubilant over being able to get home two days sooner than he had planned."

"What did he say?"

"Said he had canceled his Reno appointment and was driving straight through—and he used some little code words that meant things to us but would be meaningless to anyone else."

"These calls were more or less standard procedure?" I asked.

"Standard procedure when he'd been away," she said. "He liked to call me on long distance and hear the sound of my voice and use these little code words which sounded

31

so innocent to anyone who might be listening but which had a special meaning for us."

"What to tell them to me?" I asked.

She looked at me with a strangely direct glance and said, "What good would it do *you* to crack our code?"

"I don't want to crack it," I said, "I just want to check on it in case anyone overheard the conversation."

"I don't think it will be necessary," she said. "I know it was he who was talking, and I know he was in good spirits."

"All right, what else happened?"

"I asked him how the hitchhiker had turned out and that's when he laughed and said, 'Darling, I've got *two* hitchhikers. The *man* that I picked up at Carver City is all right, I think, but he's been drinking. But just before I got into Central Creek I picked up a really beautiful blonde.' "

"A woman?" I asked.

"A young woman hitchhiker, was the way he described her, and he laughed and said, 'I'm just ringing up to tell you that I've put her in the back seat. I think that's quite a surprise to her. I don't think she's accustomed to that sort of treatment.'

"Well, I told him to keep her in the back seat, and I told him to keep in the front seat. He laughed and told me that he would, and that he was on his way home."

"Did you ask him about what he was doing, picking up beautiful blond hitchhikers?" I asked.

She shook her head. "Of course not. Any man would have picked her up. It was around midnight and evidently this young woman, who apparently was what you would call well stacked, was thumbing a ride. My Malcolm wouldn't have passed up a dish like that. He isn't that kind—if he had been I wouldn't want him."

"Then what happened?" I asked.

"I undressed and went to bed. I slept rather soundly for four hours, then I got up and bathed and just lay there dozing.

"At about five o'clock the telephone rang. I answered

32

it, and the long-distance operator said, 'Is this Mrs. Malcolm Beckley?' I said it was and she said, 'Just a moment. I have a long-distance call for you from Rommelly, California.' Then I heard her say, 'Go ahead, please,' and a woman's voice, a very sultry voice, said, 'Mrs. Beckley?' and I said yes, and she said, 'I promised Mr. Beckley that I would telephone you. He had a flat tire and when he changed tires he found that the spare tire was also flat. I was able to hitchhike on ahead because I could catch a ride. I promised him that I'd let you know. He, of course, is staying with the car. I'm sending a repair car back to get the tire fixed. It's only ten miles.' "

"And then?" I asked.

"Then," she said, "she hung up without waiting for me to say anything—there was something rather suspicious about the whole business, the way she'd called and everything."

"And the operator told you where she was calling from?"

"Yes. It was Rommelly. I looked up Rommelly on the map and that's about sixty miles from Central Creek."

"Go on," I said.

"Well, figure it out, Mr. Lam. Suppose he was ten miles out of Rommelly. It certainly didn't take him nearly five hours to go fifty miles. The way he was feeling when I talked with him on the telephone, he could have walked fifty miles in five hours.

"Moreover, the next day I checked with Rommelly and found that neither of the agencies that send out tow cars had been called to send a repair car back along the highway for any repair at that hour of the morning. The last call that was received at one place was at three A.M. and the other place had a call at two-forty-five. I have managed to account for both of those calls; neither one of them could possibly have been my husband."

"And so?" I asked.

"Well," she said, "the picture I had at first was of my husband being very eager and very disappointed. When he had a flat tire and found that the spare was also flat, he

33

was stuck there and had to wait for a repair car. Naturally he didn't want to leave either one of the hitchhikers in his car while he went after help, and probably the man hitchhiker would have had some trouble getting help at that hour of the morning. So my husband would naturally have suggested that the blonde stand out and flag down any oncoming car and then she could have caught a ride and sent a repair car back."

I nodded.

"But that doesn't account for a five-hour delay," she went on.

"It may have taken her some time to get a ride."

"It may have," she said, "but I think there were too many impressionable males on the road and too much traffic. There were lots of fishermen on the road."

"Nevertheless," I pointed out, "a lot of motorists are pretty reluctant to stop and pick up a woman at that hour. Quite frequently holdup gangs use a good-looking woman as bait. A man brakes his car to a stop, opens the door for the woman, and suddenly a couple of men jump out of the shadows and say, 'Stick 'em up.'"

"Yes, I suppose so," she agreed. "However, that only accounts for the fact that the call came in at five o'clock. It doesn't account for the fact that more than a week has elapsed and I haven't heard a word from my husband."

"You've gone out and investigated?" I asked.

"I have not," she said. "I've sat right here with my ear glued to the telephone. I did ask the motorcycle officers to make a careful check and see if there was any evidence of a wreck between Central Creek and Bakersfield. There was no evidence of a wreck, no report of a collision of any sort. So I guess I have the answer.

"Frankly, I'm a little tired of this sort of philandering. This isn't the first time, Mr. Lam."

I raised inquiring eyebrows.

"Salesmen are peculiar people," she said. "The salesman who doesn't have a lot of drive isn't worth anything. A salesman who does . . . well, I take it you know how

34

things happen in *your* business. I daresay that half the women you meet throw themselves at you."

"Your percentage is far too high," I said.

She laughed throatily and said, "I thought you were going to say low."

"You discussed terms with Bertha Cool?" I asked.

"Certainly," she said. "Mrs. Cool fixed the price. I'm afraid she's somewhat avaricious, Mr. Lam, and also very skeptical. She wanted the money sent in by messenger. I went to the bank, got the money and sent it in by messenger."

"A joint account with your husband?" I asked.

She nodded.

"Now," I said, "suppose the remaining hitchhiker took over the car, captured your husband, drove to some secluded spot, beat him over the head and threw him out. Then what?"

"Then I'm a widow."

I met her eyes. This time she didn't glance away.

"That's right. Then you're a widow," I said.

"I think Mrs. Cool must have mentioned to you that there's an insurance policy of seventy-five thousand dollars which pays double in the event of an accidental death."

"And if he's dead, you want to establish that fact so you can collect the insurance?"

"Naturally."

"And if he's alive?"

"Then I want alimony."

"Give me his description," I said.

"Well, let's see," she said. "He has very wavy dark hair. It's not as dark as mine, sort of a brownish tint to it in certain lights, but dark. He has blue eyes and he's five feet eleven inches tall. He weighs a hundred and seventy-five pounds."

"How old?"

She hesitated a minute and said, "I've already told you he's ten years older than I am."

"How old?" I asked.

35

She said, "Isn't *anyone* entitled to secrets in dealing with a detective?"

"The information," I said, "is confidential. How old?"

"He's thirty-six."

"What kind of a car? One that's been knocked around and just has transportation left in it or—?"

"No, no!" she interrupted. "That's one thing about Malcolm. He has to have the best. He's driving a this-year model Roadracer loaded with all the accessories, adjustable seat, automatic antenna, air conditioning—the works."

"You know the license number?"

"Of course. It's NFE 801."

"You said you had a picture?"

"Two of them."

She brought out some snapshots. One of them showed a group of three men. "That's my husband," she said, "the one on the right."

I studied the picture carefully. It was pretty good for an amateur snapshot.

I held out my hand for the other one.

"I don't know whether—Could I cover up half of this and you just look at the other half?"

"You might try," I said.

She covered up half of the picture with her hand. The half I could see showed the same person I had seen in the other photograph, standing this time in a pair of bathing trunks. He was a husky individual with a slim waist, good-looking shoulders and hair on his chest. He was standing with his breath held and his shoulders squared so that it brought out his figure.

"This snapshot I can use," I said. "It's one that was taken at the beach on a day when there was a high overcast and you don't have the sharp shadows you do in the other. It gives a pretty good idea of his face."

"How did you know when it was taken?"

"Oh, you get to know a little something of photography in this business," I said. "You get so you can tell a lot about pictures just by looking at them. For instance, this picture was taken when there was a high fog but it was reasonably late in the day. It was a snapshot at a hundredth of a second and the lens was set at about f. 16. It was one of the faster films."

Her eyes widened. "How in the world can you tell all that?"

"Easy," I said. "The picture is in sharp focus. You can tell by the depth of field that the lens was stopped well down. The picture was taken at about twelve feet, and yet the background is all in focus. On the other hand, it wasn't taken with a .35 millimeter, which might account for the depth of focus. It was taken with a square camera, two and a quarter by two and a quarter, probably a twin-lensed camera since the focus is so sharp. There's just the hint of softness about the whole thing, which means that the camera moved slightly when the picture was being taken. At a two-hundred-fiftieth of a second I don't think that would have happened. It's about a hundredth-of-a-second picture."

"My cousin took it," she said. "She is a camera nut and she has a twin-lens camera just like you said. I remember she used an exposure meter and said she was shooting at a hundred at f. 16."

I nodded.

"I think it's wonderful you can tell all those things."

"I'll want to take this snapshot along," I said.

"Oh, but you couldn't!"

"Why not?"

"I'm in it."

"Phooey!" I said, and pushed her hand to one side.

She resisted a little, but it was only a token resistance.

She was wearing a Bikini bathing suit and she certainly wore it to advantage.

"Isn't that horrible!" she said. "We did it as sort of a gag."

"I don't see anything horrible about it," I said.

"It shows . . ." she averted her eyes, "too much of me."

I leaned over and studied the picture carefully.

"After all, Mr. Lam," she said coyly, "it's my husband

37

you're trying to find, not me. . . . I'm here, right here beside you."

She leaned over as though intending to take the photograph and the curve of her blouse pressed against my cheek. "Really, you mustn't have this, Mr. Lam."

"Don't be silly," I told her, "I need this picture in my business. Cut off the other half if you want, but the half with your husband I'm going to take."

"Well," she said after a moment, "I hate to cut the picture like that. You . . . you'll be careful with it, won't you?"

"Very, very careful," I told her.

"I'll have to depend on your sense of discretion."

"I don't see that you have anything to be ashamed of," I told her.

She laughed nervously and said, "Well, if I did, you could almost see it in that picture. You see, we used a homemade Bikini bathing suit and . . . you see the way the light hits it, it's almost transparent."

She put her finger on various places in the photograph.

I nodded and put the photograph in my pocket.

"Okay," I told her, "I'll get busy."

She seemed reluctant to show me to the door. "Bertha Cool told me that you were not the usual robust type one associates with investigative work but that you have a remarkable assortment of brains."

"Bertha spreads it on a little thick when she's selling my services," I said. "She's a pretty good salesman."

Daphne Beckley looked at me in mock appraisal. "I'll bet it's seventy-five per cent," she said.

"What's seventy-five per cent?"

"The women who throw themselves at you."

"You're *way* high," I said.

She said seductively, "I can well understand how they feel. You—There's something about you. . . . You inspire confidence, Mr. Lam."

"Thank you," I said with my best professional manner.

"And you arouse interest."

38

"Well," I told her, "you want to know whether you're the jilted wife of a philandering husband or a wealthy widow. I'd better get on the job and tell you which it is."

"There isn't *that* much hurry, is there?"

"There is to me," I told her, and opened the door.

5

I'VE BEEN IN THE DETECTIVE BUSINESS long enough so that I never underestimate sheer coincidence.

On the other hand, the fact that two people would disappear on the same day, that they would both send their families or friends post cards from the same service station at Carver City, and that thereafter relatives of the two people should come to the same detective agency to ask for an investigation, was a little *too* much in the way of coincidence.

I packed a suitcast, climbed in the agency heap and tooled the thing out to Carver City.

It was quite a ride. It was a hundred and eleven miles to Bakersfield, then another hundred-odd miles over winding, twisting roads. I went from the heat of the valley, winding up over tortuous grades, followed along brawling mountain streams, through timbered plateaus, skirted rocky gorges, then down on the other side losing altitude until I came to Carver City.

By that time it was eight-thirty at night.

On one side of Carver City there are wooded slopes climbing upward to high mountains which keep a cap of snow almost all summer.

On the other side and to the east the ground slopes down through foothills green during the wet season but baked hard and brown during the summer. Here there are beautiful live oak trees, then down through a more barren country until the desert shimmers in summer heat and mirages dance along the surface of the highway.

Carver City makes a big thing of the vacation trade, fishing in the spring and summer, hunting in the fall, and, of late, catering to skiing parties in the winter.

The place was jammed with motels, signs in various colored lights, sporting goods stores, restaurants and filling stations.

I found Carlyle Kamp's service station without any difficulty.

"I'm looking for the man who was on duty the fifth of the month," I said.

"What time?" the man asked.

"During the night."

"I was on duty from six o'clock in the evening until two o'clock in the morning."

"You're open all night?"

"This time of year, yes."

"How about Mr. Kamp? Does he work here?"

"He's on daytimes—not a regular shift, but he sort of runs the place and supervises what goes on."

"I've seen a few post cards sent out from the station here," I said.

"You should have," he told me. "We average about three hundred a day."

"That many?"

"That's an average. Sometimes we dish them out, it seems like, by the thousands."

"You furnish the cards free?"

"That's right."

"And the stamps?"

"And the stamps."

"Can you afford to do that?"

"Why not? It's the cheapest advertising in the world. People don't stop here to send a post card, they stop here to buy gasoline. One of our competitors down the road gives trading stamps on one company; another competitor gives trading stamps on another company. Carlyle Kamp tried to get a trading stamp concession and couldn't get one that was any good, so finally he got the idea why not give them something that will be an advertising investment and will bring in trade.

"We have those cards printed in ten thousand lots. We put on the stamps. People can't resist the opportunity to send a post card back home when it's already stamped and all they have to do is scribble on an address and a message. We have a box they can put them in for mailing."

He led me to a big wooden box that was padlocked, inserted a key in the padlock, pulled up the lid and said, "Take a look."

I looked.

Big as it was, the box was half full of post cards.

"You know what that means?" he said. "The people that come through here send out cards advertising the place. The person who gets the card sees a picture of the place. He remembers it. When he comes through here he passes up all the trading stamp bonuses and comes to the place where he gets free post cards, where he can learn all about hunting and fishing."

"You here alone?" I asked.

"Hell, no," he said. "I'm in charge, that's all. I help out when we get more than two cars at a time. The kid out there takes care of most of the chores."

He indicated a young chap in white coveralls who was washing the windshield of an automobile.

"My name's Lam," I said.

"Lennox," he told me, extending his hand. "What did you want to know about the night of the fifth?"

I said, "Are you an Elk?"

"I sure am, Bill. Where you from?"

"Fourteen thirty, Ventura," I told him.

He gave me his lodge number and we shook hands.

I said, "I wonder if you'd remember a chap who came up here and waited around for a ride on the night of the fifth, a brother Elk. He—"

"I remember him," Lennox interrupted.

"Do you know what happened to him?"

41

"I can tell you," he said, "if you really want to know and have a right to know."

I said, "I don't want this repeated but I'm a private investigator. I'm trying to find out just what happened to this party."

"Well, I can tell you," he said. "The guy was peculiar. He talked like a gentleman but he'd been on a drunk, you could see that. He hadn't been shaved, his clothes had been slept in, but—Damn it! There was something about the guy.

"Anyway, he showed up and used the rest room and started hanging around. We don't encourage people to do that. If a customer stops here and someone bums him for a ride, it's hard to refuse. Yet the driver may not want to have a passenger—I know *I* wouldn't pick up a strange man at night. It's one thing to just go whizzing by on the highway and another thing to look a man right in the eyes in a service station and tell him he can't occupy a vacant seat in your automobile.

"So when people start hanging around to ask for rides, we tell them very tactfully to be on their way, and if they don't get on their way, we put in a call for the police and they come out on what seems to be a routine checkup, pick the guy up and ask him why he shouldn't be run in for vagrancy.

"That gets the guy on the defensive, and he moves on down the road a couple of miles, which is where he should have been bumming his rides in the first place."

"But this man was different?" I asked.

"This man was different," he said, "and he was an Elk. He appealed to me as an Elk and he told a straight story. He said he was a periodic drinker, not a wino. He said he'd go all right for weeks at a time and then all of a sudden would get an urge to go out on a bender. He'd drink until his money was gone and then he'd hang around for another day or two trying to get some of his new-found friends to return some of his hospitality. When the economic pinch put a stop to his drinking, he'd gradually taper off and then all of a sudden he'd find that he was over the urge. Alcohol didn't mean a thing to him any more. He'd want to get back home, change his clothes, take a bath, be respectable; and while he'd feel shaky, he had the feeling that he never wanted to see alcohol again as long as he lived."

"You listened to his story?" I asked.

"I listened."

"What did he want?"

"He was broke flatter than a pancake. He wanted to hang around and get a ride. He didn't care particularly where he was going but he preferred Los Angeles. However, he said he'd go anywhere just so he'd be off the road at night."

"What did you do?"

"Now look," Lennox said, "Carlyle Kamp would fire me for this if he knew it. I told the guy, 'You can't proposition anyone here at this service station, but if I see a likely looking individual, I'll sound him out and ask him if he'd like to give you a lift.'

"To tell the truth, I didn't intend to talk to any person driving a passenger car. What I wanted was some fellow with a beat-up pickup or something of that sort who was looking for company.

"However, after the guy had been here for about ten minutes, a pickup came in, and I asked the man if he wanted company. I told him to tell me frankly. The guy said he didn't. He said he'd been turning down hitchhikers all along the road. He'd never seen so many of them."

"So then what?" I asked.

"Well, it must have been about ten minutes later a guy drove up in a car that looked like a million dollars. It was loaded—one swell job, and right out of a clear sky he asked me."

"Asked you what?"

"Asked me . . . well, he didn't actually ask me either, but he told me that he had a long drive ahead of him and he was fighting off sleep. He said he was going to pick up someone to help him drive the car."

"How did he happen to tell you that?"

43

"Frankly," Lennox said, "I think it was because he saw this man back out there just on the fringe of the lighted area."

"So what did you do?"

"I told the guy that a fellow had been around here a half-hour ago looking for a ride and I thought he was still around someplace. I told the customer that if he *really* wanted someone to help him drive, I might be able to find this fellow, and the customer said he really wanted someone. He said he was headed for Reno."

"You don't remember the name of this Elk, do you?"

"Frankly, I don't. He came up and flashed his card on me and gave me his lodge number and we shook hands. I didn't know what he wanted at the time, I thought it was a touch and I'd made up my mind to tell him there were ten million Elks, more or less, in the United States and that on my salary I couldn't take care of my wife and kid, let alone support a whole lodge."

"And then?"

"Well, then this fellow driving the car said he'd sure like to talk with this guy and size him up so he could see if he wanted to take a chance on him. I told him I'd look around—I walked around the service station and beckoned to the guy who was sitting out there in the shadows, and he came over and he and this fellow got talking, and I guess the hitchhiker made a good impression because the fellow loaded him into his car and he drove off."

"And you wouldn't have any idea who that fellow was?" I asked.

He grinned at me and said, "Now there, my friend, is where I fool you—I just got worrying a little bit about maybe being a pushover and I got wondering what would happen if—well, you know, if anything did happen.

"Well, this fellow was driving a loaded Roadracer, one swell automobile and he looked like a million dollars. He was well dressed—anyhow, I took down his license number."

"You've still got it?"

44

"Look, Lam, what's this all about?"

I met his eyes and said, "I don't know. Maybe something, maybe nothing, but holding out information isn't going to help any and it may hurt a lot."

"Hurt who?"

"You."

He thought it over and said, "Look, will you do me a favor? Will you keep this thing just between us unless you find you *have* to tell—I mean keep me out of it?"

"I'm not broadcasting information at the moment," I said.

"What happened?" he asked. "Did this fellow turn out to be no good? He didn't try a holdup, did he?"

"I don't think so," I said, "but I don't know. Right at the present time I'd just like to have him as a witness."

"But what did he do?"

"Perhaps nothing," I said.

"You're not telling me much."

"Look, I'm an investigator, Lennox. I'm paid to get information, not to give it. If you want news, read your newspaper, tune in on your television or your radio but don't ask a man who's gathering information for a living to give it out for nothing."

"But you're asking *me* for a favor."

"I'm calling on you for information that you have. It's information you're going to have to give. You can either give it to me the easy way or I can get it the hard way. If you give it to me now, there's a good possibility Carlyle Kamp will never hear anything about it. If you make me do it the hard way, there's a damned good chance your local newspaper will have the story in the morning edition."

"What did this guy do?"

"Perhaps nothing. Frankly, my interest is more with the man who was driving the Roadracer."

"How did you know he stopped here?"

I indicated the rack of stamped post cards with a big sign above the cards: STAMPED SOUVENIR POST CARDS FREE ALL READY FOR MAILING. HELP YOURSELF.

That made him feel better. He said, "Okay, let me see if I can find that license number. I kept it around for a few days thinking I'd have it in case anything happened. When I didn't hear anything I intended to put it in the wastebasket but I don't think I did. I think it's in the cash register somewhere."

He went back and rang up No Sale on the cash register, took a key from his pocket, opened a little locked compartment, rummaged around through some paper money, then shook his head and said, "I'm sorry, Lam. I don't think I can— Wait a minute, wait a minute, here it is."

He pulled out a slip of paper. On it had been scrawled the words, Roadracer, late model, license number NFE 801.

"This is in your handwriting?" I said.

He nodded.

I turned it over and said, "Write the date on there—the date you wrote it down. That was the fifth."

He nodded and put the date on there.

"Now," I said, "put down this date and put your initials."

He did as I requested. I put the slip of paper in my notebook.

"If that means anything," he said, "I think *I* should keep it."

"It doesn't mean that much," I told him. "*I'm* keeping it— Think you'd recognize these people if you saw them again?"

"You mean the hitchhiker and the guy who gave him the ride?"

I nodded.

"I think so," he said. "I remember the guy in the Roadracer had a credit card—we honor all credit cards here. Now I don't remember just what company had issued the credit card, but we could probably go back in the records and find out if it became that important."

"It isn't that important," I told him, and then after a moment added, "yet."

"You can't tell me what happened?"

"As far as I know, nothing happened."

"But why are you investigating?"

"Because I have a client who asked me to make the investigation."

"And what does your client want to know?"

"All I can find out."

He grinned and just then a couple of cars came in at once. There was one car already at the pumps so Lennox said, "Okay, Lam, give me the breaks if you can. Remember I've come clean with you. I've got to go work on these cars."

He went over to the pumps, and I went over to the rack of post cards, picked out one and addressed it to Bertha Cool at the agency.

"Having a fine time," I wrote. "Wish you were here—actually you should make the trip, Bertha. It's a unique service station. The post cards are all stamped and they're all free. You can send as many as you want—why not drop in a few days before Christmas."

I signed the card and stuck it in the wooden box.

People from the cars that were being serviced started milling around. One of them went into one of the air-conditioned phone booths to telephone, some of the others went over to the post card rack and helped themselves to post cards.

I wondered how much the cards actually cost the guy—evidently they brought in business, because half a dozen cars had been driven in while I had been talking. On the other hand, the brightly lit service station half a block down the street that was advertising all sorts of bonus propositions had only serviced one car during the same period.

I was sleepy but I still had work to do so I climbed in the car, drove up to an all-night restaurant, had two cups of black coffee and started back up the grade.

Central Creek was twenty miles from Carver City. There wasn't much more than a general merchandise store,

47

a barnlike structure which had "Garage" painted on it, a couple of service stations, and a small café.

There was a telephone booth in the restaurant. I went in and had a sandwich and a cup of coffee.

The girl who waited on me was a blonde who had lots of curves and knew it.

"I'm trying to find out something about a man who used the phone here on the night of the fifth," I said. "Were you on duty?"

She smiled and shook her head, "I can't help you a bit, Mister."

"You don't remember him?"

"I didn't come here until the morning of the sixth. Then's when I started to work."

"What happened to the girl whose place you took?" I asked.

"Nothing," she said with a smile, "that's why she left."

"Thanks," I told her.

I was beginning to get a picture. Malcolm Beckley had filled up his car at Carlyle Kamp's service station in Carver City. There were some good eating places in Carver City.

Then he'd gone on to Central Creek and had stopped.

The restaurant in Central Creek wasn't particularly inviting. It was only twenty miles from Carver City and as yet the real mountain grades hadn't started. A man could make those twenty miles in twenty-two or twenty-three minutes without any trouble, twenty-seven or twenty-eight minutes would be slow driving.

Malcolm Beckley had passed up the good restaurants in Carver City but had eaten half an hour later.

The answer seemed obvious. Malcolm Beckley hadn't been particularly hungry but during that half-hour he'd picked up his second hitchhiker, a well-stacked blonde. One or the other of these hitchhikers had been hungry, so Beckley had stopped at this café to give them something to eat. He hadn't been hungry himself or he'd have eaten at one of the good cafés in Carver City.

So while his hitchhikers were grabbing a quick cup of coffee and a sandwich at this little place at Central Creek,

Beckley had decided to call his wife to tell her the Reno trip was off and he'd be home.

One thing was certain, Beckley had been eager to get home and he hadn't waited around for any cooking to be done. The blonde hitchhiker and Amos Gage must have had to grab coffee and doughnuts or a sandwich, Beckley had phoned, and then they'd been on their way.

So far, so good.

The waitress who had been on duty might have remembered one well-dressed man accompanied by another man who was slightly unkempt and needed a shave, and a well-stacked blonde. The well-dressed man went to the telephone while the others were eating.

Moreover, the waitress might have remembered some of the conversation.

"Where could I find this girl who was here before you?" I asked.

The waitress shook her head.

"Who runs the place?" I asked.

"Dorothy Lennox."

"Miss or Mrs?"

"Mrs."

"Any relation to Frank Lennox down at Carlyle Kamp's service station?"

"She's his wife. She runs this restaurant and owns the general merchandising store. He works at Kamp's in Carver City."

"Where can I find Mrs. Lennox?"

"She's in Los Angeles someplace, doing some buying."

"You met this girl when you took over—the waitress whose place you took?"

"No, she was gone before I got here. I just happened along. Mrs. Lennox was waiting on the tables herself. She talked me into taking over, at least temporarily."

"Who does the cooking?" I asked.

"Pops!" she called.

A wizened individual with a somewhat rumpled chef's cap stuck his head up over the partition in the back.

"Huh?" he asked.

"Man out here wants to know who does the cooking," the waitress said.

"I do," Pops said, and looked at me. "What do you want?"

"To know who does the cooking," I told him.

"You know now," he said and ducked back out of sight.

"Come on back, Pops," I called. "There are two bucks you didn't wait for. Here they are."

I took out two one-dollar bills.

The head popped back into view. A twisted grin showed some snags of yellowed teeth. He stretched out an eager hand for the money.

I got the idea he might have been in prison and had learned his cooking in stir.

"Who was cooking on the night of the fifth?"

"I was."

"Remember a man who brought in a couple of hitch-hikers, one rather seedy looking and the other a blonde, and who was probably in a big hurry?"

"Sure do. That is, I remember the man who was in one hell of a rush. There were two orders of ham and eggs. He finally agreed to wait, but told me to hurry it up. The big shot went to the phone and put through a call. He kept hurrying things up—that's why I remembered him. He sure made his two friends gulp their food.

"Anything more I can do for you? Figure you got your two bucks' worth?"

I handed him another two dollars and gave one to the waitress. "Just remember what you've told me," I said to Pops. "It may get you some more money. Do you remember the woman?"

"Never got a look at her," Pops said and grinned at the recollection.

"They kept me busy cooking those ham and eggs. Afterward I guess I could have seen 'em while they was eating but I was interested in the man. He was standing where you are. I'd know him again. The other guy and the woman were over in the corner. The woman had her back to me."

I thanked them both and went out.

Rommelly was up in the mountains, another sixty miles of twisting road. It was hard-surfaced but slow driving. I drove along slowly, looking for anything my headlights might pick up which would be a clue.

All I found were empty beer cans and broken glass.

Rommelly was a fair sized little town, but it rolled up the sidewalks and went to bed at night. There were two garages in the place. Each place had a pushbutton on the front labeled "Night bell."

I rang the night bell on the place nearest the east end of town. It took about five minutes and three separate rings before the door opened.

A man about twenty-seven with wavy blond hair, sleep-swollen blue eyes, wearing only a pair of shorts, was struggling into a pair of pants as he opened the door.

"What's the trouble?" he asked in a voice that was still thick with sleep.

"I'd like to talk with you," I said.

"Talk!" he exclaimed, "Where's your car?"

"Outside."

"What's wrong with it?"

"Nothing."

"Say, what the hell!"

I took a half-pint of whiskey from my hip pocket.

He looked the whiskey bottle over. The seals were intact. A slow grin spread over his face. "That's different," he said. "Come on in."

He led me back to the corner in a partitioned-off room where his cot was located.

There were no sheets on the bed. The blankets showed evidence of considerable use. There was a slip on the pillow, but it had been a long time since it had seen a laundry.

Back of the cot were pin-up pictures on the wall. Some of them were conventional pin-ups which had been clipped from magazines. There were a couple of nudes evidently taken from a magazine featuring photographic studies of the nude figure, and there was one glossy photograph of a girl completely in the nude turned sideways to the camera, looking over her shoulder with a provocative smile.

He sat down on the cot and shoved the flask of whiskey under the soiled pillowslip.

I asked him about a call from a blonde sometime during the night of the fifth or the morning of the sixth.

He shook his head emphatically. "Some dame was asking about that on the telephone," he said. "She telephoned the boss and asked him, and he put me on the phone. I talked with her. There wasn't any call like that."

I sized him up and decided that the possibility he would forget a call from a well-stacked blonde was about as likely as expecting a hungry lion to overlook a chunk of beef that was tossed into the cage.

I shook hands and left.

The other garage with a night bell was operated by a man about thirty-five who didn't warm up at all. He accepted the whiskey, but his eyes were hard and hostile.

"You a cop?" he asked.

"An investigator," I told him.

"Same thing," he said.

I didn't debate the point. I asked him about the call.

He, too, shook his head. "What the hell's the idea of getting me up in the middle of the night to ask me about that?" he demanded. "I've already told the boss all I know about it. There wasn't any such call. There wasn't any dame. You hear me? There wasn't any dame. Now beat it!"

I tried one more question. "Are you sure you'd have remembered it if—?"

"Of course I would have remembered it," he said. "Would a guy on a desert island forget it if a strip-tease queen washed up on the beach at daylight—don't be silly! What's more, Copper, I keep a record of calls. Every time that night bell rings there's a tape punched. I make a note on my book every time I answer that doorbell.

"The boss is an electrician. There's a paper tape run

52

by clockwork. You push that button and the mechanism punches the tape, showing the time. When I open this door, it makes another punch on the tape.

"If somebody pushes the button and I don't answer, the tape shows a punch with no corresponding opening of the door. If I take as much as five minutes to open the door, it shows on the tape.

"That's the kind of a goddam boss I've got. Now beat it, Copper!"

"I'm not a copper," I said.

"Same thing," he said and slammed the door, taking the half-pint of whiskey with him.

I wrote that place off the books. The electric tape and the signal seemed to cover the answer there.

But what would have happened if a well-stacked blonde had rung the bell at the other place in the middle of the night, the sleepy attendant stumbled to the door pulling on his pants . . . and then what?

One thing seemed pretty certain. No matter what had happened, Beckley hadn't received any help. He'd been left out there, flat tire and all.

That meant that he stayed there until the tire got fixed. The probabilities were the spare tire hadn't had a puncture but had a slow leak probably from a defective valve. Possibly some passing motorist had seen Beckley's predicament and stopped to help. He could have had a tire pump and they'd pumped up the spare tire so Beckley could keep on traveling.

In that case he'd have gone right on through Rommelly, presumably still accompanied by the male hitchhiker. The blond hitchhiker would have fallen by the wayside somewhere. She could have secured a ride and gone on ahead. She could have phoned Mrs. Beckley and said she was sending a tow car back when for reasons of her own she'd never even gone near one of the garages.

On the other hand, why had it taken so long from the time Beckley left Central Creek before he arrived at a point some ten miles out of Rommelly?

Or, if the two hitchhikers had got together and bashed

in Beckley's head and taken his car, why wouldn't it have been a smart thing for the blonde to have put in that phone call about the flat tire as a blind? The effect of that call would have been to take the heat off the blonde in case of any investigation such as I was making.

I found a motel with a vacancy sign at Rommelly and rolled in for a few hours' shut-eye.

Shortly after daylight I was on the road again. This time I crawled along the mountain grades, looking for any sign that a car might have gone off into the canyon. First I went thirty miles back toward Central Creek, then I turned back, drove to Rommelly and then drove slowly to Bakersfield.

There was no sign of any accident I could see, not even a freshly splintered section on a guardrail.

Several times I stopped the car at likely-looking places, got out and looked down over a sharp drop to a mountain creek. I couldn't see any sign of a car, any freshly broken bits of shrubbery or dislodged rocks.

It was after nine o'clock by the time I got to Bakersfield.

I telephoned Mrs. Beckley.

Her voice sounded sleepy.

"Donald Lam," I said. "I'm calling from Bakersfield. Did your husband have any samples with him in his car?"

"He worked mostly with photographs," she said. "Where are you, Mr. Lam?"

"In Bakersfield."

"When are you coming in to . . . to report to me?"

"Not for a while," I said. "How about money? Your husband carried a goodly sum of money?"

"He always had enough for emergencies, but mostly he relied on traveler's checks."

"What kind of checks?"

"American Express Company," she said.

"Did he keep any record of the numbers of the traveler's checks he had?"

She thought for a moment and then said suddenly, "Why

54

yes! I believe he did. There's a little black book that contains some records."

"Go get the little black book," I said, "and remember I'm on long distance."

"Just a minute, Donald," she said.

She slipped into the first-name basis with easy familiarity and made it sound as though she had been calling me Donald all of her life.

It was no more than a minute before she was back.

She read off a list of numbers.

Evidently Malcolm Beckley had about five hundred dollars of uncashed traveler's checks in denominations ranging from fifty dollars to twenty dollars.

I thanked her, told her I was making "progress," hung up and put through more long-distance calls.

A friend of mine on the police force agreed to get in touch with the American Express Company right away and see if any checks with numbers corresponding to those carried by Beckley had been cashed within the last ten days.

One thing about the police, when they want to they can get results, and one thing about the American Express Company, they're efficient.

I had a late and leisurely breakfast, sat in the lobby of a motel, read the papers and then called my friend on the police force to give him the name of the motel where I could be reached.

He had results. One fifty-dollar check had been cashed within the last four days. It had been cashed by a casino in Reno, Nevada.

I didn't bother to call Daphne Beckley. I simply gassed up the car and headed for Reno.

I had one batch of mechanical trouble with the agency heap but got it straightened out after a while. It was night by the time I reached Reno.

The place where the check had been cashed was going full blast with all the synthetic glitter of a Nevada gambling establishment.

This was one of the most sumptuous places in the

whole outfit. Heaven knows how many slot machines were in operation. Many of them were being played by women.

For some strange reason the so-called one-armed bandit is the woman's method of gambling.

Despite the hundreds of slot machines running through five cents, ten cents, twenty-five cents, fifty cents and silver dollars, it was difficult to get a machine that wasn't in play.

There were a few fifty-cent machines and one or two dollar machines which were idle, but the ten-cent machines were getting the bulk of the play, and the twenty-five-cent machines were nearly all in use.

In lots of places players were keeping two machines in operation, putting a coin in the slot, pulling down the arm of one machine, then jumping over to the other machine, putting in a coin, pulling down the arm, and then returning to the first machine as the signals clicked into place. One woman, in fact, was holding down three ten-cent machines, working with a steady rhythm which indicated a skill born of long practice. She might have been a piece worker in a factory with every motion figured out by an efficiency expert so she could get the most out of her time. If she'd have had to work that hard, she'd have been headed for a nervous breakdown, but because she was "having fun," her eyes were alert and she was moving from one machine to another like a mechanical part of the establishment itself.

I wanted to look the place over and size it up a bit before tipping my hand.

Back of the slot machines were all sorts of gambling devices: roulette, blackjack, faro, craps, chuck-a-luck, and wheels of fortune.

The place was jammed. Every so often the slot machines would pay off, and coins would come rattling down into the metal cups, keeping a steady tinkle of encouragement to spur on the devotees.

I took an escalator to the second floor, then on up to the third floor.

It was quite a place. Slot machines everywhere. Sharp-eyed dolls with keen, busy eyes but features and figures that were easy on the eyes, circulated around with coin dispensers strapped on their bodies in such a way as not to interfere with the natural contours.

I changed a five-dollar bill into quarters. The willowy young woman simply pushed the five-dollar bill into a pocket, pressed a lever, and twenty quarters came cascading out into the palm of her hand.

She transferred the quarters to my hand. "Good luck," she said, smiling.

I played for about twenty-minutes, sometimes ahead of the game, sometimes behind. Then I got down to the last four quarters.

I saw a little glass window with a sign over it, "The Prospector's Vision, twenty-five cents."

I dropped in a quarter and put my eyes up against the dark window.

For a moment everything was dark, but I thought I could hear the whirring of concealed mechanism somewhere—then it began to get light.

It was a wonderful diorama of the desert.

There were mountains in the far background, and the exhibit was so cunningly displayed that it looked as though it must have been twenty miles back to those mountains. A little steely daylight began to creep into the sky. It rapidly changed to the red of dawn, and a big saguaro was outlined against the sky. Then the light grew in intensity, and the foreground began to materialize.

Lying in the foreground was a nude woman.

I knew she was made out of wax or plastic or something but it was *most* realistic. She looked to be about six feet away and all she wore was a pleasant smile on her face and a red silk handkerchief loosely tied about her waist.

The light grew stronger. The flesh-colored contours assumed pleasing proportions. Then from somewhere a vagrant breeze sprang up. The red silk fluttered a couple of times, then as the breeze swept across the face of the desert, the red silk blew straight up for one tantalizing instant just as the lights went out and the place was dark again.

It was a masterpiece of illusion.

I dropped another quarter of Bertha Cool's expense money and watched the thing all over again.

I contemplated dropping another quarter but decided against it. I turned away, and a soft feminine voice touched with amusement said, "Not quitting so soon, are you?"

I looked her over. She might have been up there to take the "cure" as the locals describe it.

Under the Nevada law six weeks is all the residence that is necessary to give the courts jurisdiction in a divorce action. Hearings are prompt and the decrees are final. Once they go into effect parties can remarry immediately. Locals call the six-week residence period "taking the cure."

"There's something wrong with the lighting," I said. "The lights always go off at the psychological moment."

"Too bad," she said, and smiled archly. "Perhaps that's because you're only playing quarters."

"Gosh!" I said, "I never thought of that . . . but there's no place where you could put anything bigger."

"Such as a fifty-cent piece?" she asked.

"Or a twenty-dollar bill," I suggested.

"I'll have to speak to the management about that," she told me. "Are you playing the machines?"

"I have been. How about you?"

"I have been."

"Why did you quit?"

"Why did *you*?"

"I liked the scenery in the Prospector's Vision," I said.

She said, "I ran out of money."

"Perhaps," I told her, "you need some lucky money."

"Perhaps I do."

I called over an attendant and handed her another five-dollar bill.

The girl leaned against me. "The management won't stand for touches," she said. "This girl saw me alone earlier in the evening. I'll see you later."

She drifted away.

58

The attendant who had handed me the twenty quarters moved around, apparently paying little attention to me, but every time I moved away I saw her watching me.

I put four quarters in the two-bit machine and on the fourth quarter hit the jackpot.

The attendant was right at my elbow.

I tried a fifty-cent machine and won sixteen dollars on the third try.

I moved casually around.

The young woman who had spoken to me was watching me with surreptitious but hungry eyes.

I took the escalator down to the main floor and waited for a moment to see if she showed up.

She didn't.

I didn't know whether she'd changed her mind or whether the management had done something about enforcing its edict against panhandlers.

After a while the whole thing seemed garish and monotonous. I realized I was tired. I went over to the cashier. "Look," I said, "I'm a private investigator. I'd like to trace an American Express traveler's check that went through here a little over a week ago."

"How much was it?"

"Fifty dollars."

She looked at me as though I might have been crazy. "Over a week ago?"

"Around that."

"Do you know how much money goes through this place in twenty-four hours?"

I shook my head.

"I'd be fired if I told you," she said. "Do you have any idea the size of the stack of checks that goes to the bank every day?"

Again I shook my head.

"All right," she said, "go get a cup of coffee and quit bothering me about a fifty-dollar check that came through here a week ago. You might as well go out on the street when it's snowing and ask me if I've seen a particular snowflake."

Then suddenly her features softened with a smile. "I'd like to help you," she said, "honestly," and her smile was friendly, cordial and personal. Then someone came up to cash a check. Her smile remained cordial, her eyes became as hard as an adding machine.

"Do you have something in the way of personal identification?" she asked the guy who was holding out the check.

I moved away.

An early breakfast in Reno is an adventure in itself.

My breakfast was just before daylight. A couple of girls who might have been professional shills for a gambling game, or a couple of divorcees pooling their fortunes and misfortunes, or a couple of tourists who had been in search of adventure and failed, were eating scrambled eggs and toast with the listless dejection of women who know that no matter what else the world may hold, there are no longer any dreams or illusions.

A chap who looked as though he might be a professional panhandler, but who probably had a million dollars, was chewing food with rhythmic regularity—just taking aboard fuel for the day and apparently having no idea what the stuff tasted like.

There were some tourists getting an early start, a man who had evidently done all right for himself at the casinos, who was all pepped up with flushed face and bright eyes despite the early morning hour. There were a couple of gambling dealers going off duty and a man in the uniform of a service station employee gulping his food with one eye on his watch.

I got out of the restaurant just as it was light enough to see and started down the highway, making a round of the motels.

It was a long, tedious procedure. I'd drive in one motel, completely circle the thing looking for Roadracers with a California license, then I'd turn into the next place, repeat the performance and so on down the road. After I came to the last motel on the west side of the road, I turned back toward Reno and started checking the motels on the east.

It was such a hopeless procedure that despite myself I had a hard time keeping alert. It's easy to miss a car when you're seeing them by the hundreds.

Then suddenly I did a double take, looked back for a third time, and slammed on the brakes.

It was a Roadracer sedan, and the California license number was NFE 801.

I pulled my car off to the side where it would be out of the way, parked it, put the key in my pocket and walked back to look the car over. It was parked in an enclosure beside Cabin Number 12. It showed no signs of having been in any accident.

I walked up to Cabin 12 and knocked on the door.

There was no answer.

I knocked again.

A sleepy voice said, "Huh? What is it?"

I said, "Open up."

The voice was more alert this time. "What do you want?"

"Insurance company," I said. "I'm investigating the Roadracer, license number NFE 801. Is that your car?"

There was no answer for several long seconds. Then I heard feet on the floor, and the door was unlocked.

The man who stood in the door was about thirty-five, somewhere around five feet eleven, with blue eyes and wavy dark hair that had a brownish tinge. He took me in with a survey of sleep-swollen eyes, then looked past me as though expecting to find the police. When he saw that I was alone, some of the apprehension left him.

"Who are you?"

"I'll explain that," I said, and pushed forward.

For a split second I felt he might be going to try to keep me from entering. Then he stood to one side and I went in.

"Better get some clothes on," I said.

He welcomed the opportunity to get his thoughts together. He had been sleeping in undershirt and shorts,

61

and he put on trousers, shirt, socks and shoes, belted the trousers, went to the bathroom, washed his face and hands, came out drying himself with a towel, took a comb from his pocket and ran it through his hair.

"Thought one up yet?" I asked.

"What do you mean?"

"A good story."

"Why should I think up a story?"

"What's your name?"

He hesitated a moment, then said, "Malcolm G. Beckley."

"What's your wife's first name?" I asked him.

He looked at me, blinked, and then suddenly caved in and sat down on the edge of the bed as though his knees wouldn't support him any more.

"Ever know anyone by the name of Amos Gage?" I asked.

"You win," he said.

"Go on," I told him.

"I knew it was coming," he said wearily. "My God, Officer, if I'd only known what to do. If I'd only had someone to talk with—however, I had to try to play it alone and I made a mess of things."

"How much property did you steal from Beckley?" I asked.

"I didn't steal any."

"Don't be silly," I told him.

He didn't say anything.

"It was such a damn-fool caper," I went on. "Here you are about to come into a fortune if you don't get convicted of crime and then you go and lead with your chin."

"It isn't that way at all," he said. "I . . . I just got put in a position where I didn't know what to do and for a while I didn't know who I was."

"Amnesia, eh?"

"For a while."

I laughed.

"It's the truth, I tell you. It's the honest truth. I've

read about those things happening but I never knew they really could happen that way. It sure happened to me."

"Go on," I said skeptically, "let's hear your story, but don't waste time trying to embellish it. I hear these things so often they get nauseating after a while. However, you can try it out on me and it will be good practice. Then when you tell it in court you will at least have had a little rehearsal."

"In court!" he exclaimed.

"Sure," I said. "Where did *you* think?"

He was silent for a while, thinking, apparently debating whether he should clam up.

"Well," I said impatiently, "go ahead, start talking. Let's hear what it sounds like."

When he still hesitated I said, "It'll probably do you good to get it off your chest anyway. You'll feel better."

That rang a bell.

He said, "My name is Amos Gage, as you well know. I guess I don't amount to much. I go on periodic drunks. I don't know why. I'll get along all right for a while and then the craving gets me."

I yawned.

"I've always tried to keep from doing anything that would get me in trouble," he said. "I never carry over a hundred and fifty dollars with me and the minute I take my first drink I mail the car keys to a friend and then I'm on foot. By the time I've gone through the money I have on me, I start sobering up. Sometimes I go on a short toot, sometimes it's longer."

"Never mind the generalities," I told him, "tell me about Beckley."

"All right," he said. "I'd been on a drunk. I don't know how long it was. I guess I must have found someone who held up his end and did some of the buying because I think it was a pretty long one."

"Who was your companion?" I asked, "Beckley?"

"Hell no," he said. "I didn't know who he was. All I know is that I finally began to sober up. I was flat broke. I didn't even have the price of a cup of coffee in my pocket. I guess I'd been rolled—and I sure wanted coffee. I was in one hell of a state."

"Go on," I said.

"I have a system of getting home when I'm recovering from one of these drunks. I go to a drinking fountain, load up with all the water I can get and then when I get to feeling a little less shaky, I walk out to where there are some pretty good service stations and look around until I find someone who is a brother Elk."

"And then?"

"Then I appeal to him as a brother Elk. I'm in distress. I ask for help. I want to get a ride home. Usually the guy helps me. Sometimes he'll even stake me to the price of a cup of coffee and a meal."

"This time?" I asked.

"This time," he said, "the fellow told me to get out of the light and away from the service station but not to go away, to stick around and wait and he'd see what could be done."

"Remember the fellow's name?" I asked.

"Frankly I don't. All I know is the place was Carver City. At the time I knew his name. He gave me his lodge number and we shook hands. But that's about all I can do. I could go to Carver City and find the service station and of course I'd recognize the fellow if I saw him again.

"This place had give-away post cards all stamped for mailing. It was an advertising gimmick. I wrote a post card to this friend of mine, saying I was all right and was on my way home."

I let myself show interest. There was something in the guy's manner that indicated sincerity. "What happened next?" I asked.

"I'd been there about half an hour," he said. "The service station attendant came over to me and said, 'Look, Buddy, I'm getting you a ride. I'm leaving it up to you not to let me down. I'm putting it up to you on the basis of loyalty to the lodge'—well, I shook hands with him and told him he'd never regret it, that I was on the up and up. I told him a little about myself.

64

"He told me there was a fellow there who was going to Reno and who was going to have to drive most of the night. He was looking for a relief driver."

"Go on," I said.

"The service station man took me over and introduced me to this fellow. I didn't get his name at the time, of course. It was just a man who was going to Reno who was willing to take me along. He was driving this Road-racer.

"I didn't particularly want to go to Reno. I wanted to go to Los Angeles, but I had butterflies in my stomach and I didn't want to spend the night on the road. I'd have settled for anything just so I could have some coffee and ham and eggs. I knew this chap would buy me food sooner or later and I'd be off the road and going places. Anything was better than spending the night by the side of the highway. And the roads sure were full of people wanting rides. I don't know why it was. Some fruit-picking season had just ended or something. The roads were full of hitchhikers."

"Go on," I said.

"Well, this fellow put through some phone calls and then told me his plans had changed and he was headed for Los Angeles and was that all right with me."

"Was it all right? Hell, I could have kissed the guy. He said we'd drive straight through to Los Angeles."

"Go on," I told him.

"I got in the car with him and of course I knew from what the service station attendant had told me that this fellow wanted me to do some of the driving, but I wasn't going to push myself forward. I could see that he was studying me a bit and after a while he asked me if I was a wino. I told him the truth. I told him that I went on a periodic drunk once in a while and then woke up broke and had to hitchhike home, that I was cold sober but I was a little jittery and I told him I hadn't eaten for a spell. So he told me that was fine and that he'd stop at the next town and get me some hot coffee and then he'd put me behind the wheel and see how I was doing and whether

I was a good driver—and then this woman was out in the road."

"What woman?"

"Another hitchhiker, and boy, was *she* a knockout!"

"Who was she?"

"I don't know. She said to call her Madge and that was all either one of us ever found out—at least as far as I know."

"All right, what happened?"

"She used her thumb, and he stopped the car and talked with her for a minute, asked her where she was going and she said Los Angeles. He asked her what she was doing hitchhiking and she started making smart cracks. She told him that she was putting on too much weight and her doctor had advised her to take long walks, that she figured about three hundred miles was far enough and she also told him that she was a fugitive from the wolf pack. Well, anyway he told her to get in and then he sort of apologized. He told her that I was going to be doing the driving after we passed the next town so she was going to have to sit in the back seat, and she said that was all right with her. She had been fighting off guys who wanted to paw her until her skin was rubbed raw—she was quite some girl."

"Quick on the uptake?" I asked.

"I'll say she was quick, and boy, she was a number!"

"All right, what happened?"

"Well, we got to the next city, Central Creek, and he stopped and let us get something to eat. We had ham and eggs but we sure had to gulp them. While we were eating, the fellow went over to the phone and called somebody long distance. I don't know who it was. I think he was calling home."

"Did he deposit any money or was it a collect call?" I asked.

"I don't know. I think—Wait a minute, he deposited money. I remember that now, but I guess that was just to get the operator."

"Wouldn't he have called home collect?" I asked.

"Hell, I don't know," Gage said irritably. "I'm telling you what happened. It's one hell of a story. Just keep on listening. You haven't heard anything yet."

"I'm listening," I said.

"All right. We started out from Central Creek. Beckley told me that he'd wait a little while for the food to put a little warmth into my blood and then he'd let me take over at the wheel."

"Where was the woman?"

"In the back seat. She said she could drive, but Beckley pretended he didn't hear her, so then she sat tight and kept quiet."

"All right," I said. "You had a flat tire and—"

"Huh?" he said, looking at me.

"A flat tire and then he jacked up the car and when he put on the spare he found that it was flat and—"

Gage was shaking his head violently.

"No?" I asked.

"No," he said.

"All right, what did happen?"

"I don't know."

"What do you mean?"

"We were driving along and all of a sudden the roof caved in on me. I went out like a light. I remember the shock of a blow and I was sick all over before the blackness came over me. I have a feeling I may have been hit twice but I don't know."

"Did Beckley hit you?"

"He was driving. It must have been the woman, but I don't know. I tell you, the world just caved in. The ceiling fell on me."

"Then what?" I asked.

"I woke up and it was still dark. I was lying by this automobile, the right front door was open. I was flat on the ground. Blood had been running down my neck, and the shoulder of my coat had some blood on it. I didn't know where I was, and honest to God, Mister, I didn't know *who* I was. All I knew was that there was some sort of a blind panic making me want to get away from there fast."

"What did you do?"

"The headlights were on, the motor was running, and almost without knowing what I did, I got to my feet, had a couple of dizzy spells, leaned against the car, then slid into the front seat and, as I say, all of a sudden this panic hit me. I knew I had to get away from there fast."

"What did you do?"

"I drove the car along a dirt road and then I came to a paved road after a couple of miles. I don't know where it was, it was downhill to the right, uphill to the left. I just turned the car to the left going uphill and poured the gas into it. I had the funniest damn feeling, I just didn't know who I was. Everything was a complete blank to me. I couldn't remember a thing about my past life or anything. I was just driving a car."

"You knew how to drive the car?"

"I knew how to drive," he said, "but I just couldn't remember anything that had happened. I might just as well have been born right there by the side of that car."

"What did you do?"

"I kept driving on, thinking that my memory would come to me. It didn't. I stopped at a restaurant and got coffee. I felt in my pockets and there was money. I paid for the coffee. I went into the rest room, locked the door and started taking stock of myself. I had a wallet with a driving license made to Malcolm G. Beckley. I had some of Beckley's cards, some identification papers, and there was money in the wallet, a little over a hundred dollars. I had a book of traveler's checks in denominations ranging from twenty dollars to fifty dollars. It was a new book. Nothing had been cashed from it and those were Malcolm Beckley checks. That is, they were made to Malcolm Beckley—you know how traveler's checks are. You sign your name when you get them and you sign your name again when you cash them."

"So what did you do?"

"Well, I naturally assumed I was Malcolm Beckley and

I started driving again. I had a vague idea I should go to Los Angeles, but I didn't have the faintest idea where Los Angeles was. I didn't know *where* I was, I didn't know anything except I knew how to drive a car. I kept on driving, thinking that memory would come back to me but it didn't.

"I did know there was something behind me I was running away from and it was something that frightened the hell out of me. I kept looking at the back road in the rearview mirror without quite knowing what it was I was looking for. And then I got afraid to stay on the main road. This fear of what was behind me led me to turn off on a good-looking graveled road to the right and then I found myself on a lot of winding mountain roads. I just kept driving without knowing who I was, where I was, or where I was going.

"At last I began to get down out of the mountains. Then I hit paved road again. Finally I saw a road sign and realized that I was on the road to Reno. I didn't know where Reno was. It could have been a suburb of Los Angeles for all I knew. One place was just like another as far as I was concerned."

"You didn't stop and ask for directions?"

"Hell, no. I was terribly afraid that something was wrong. I had an instinctive fear. I kept on driving, and then I came to Reno.

"I might just as well have been starting life all over again except I knew certain things. I knew how to shoot crap, I knew how to play roulette, I knew how to drive a car, I knew all of the things you have to do in everyday life."

"So what did you do?"

"I gambled up the money I had. For a while I was lucky and then I became unlucky. And then I was broke."

"So then what?"

"Then I cashed a traveler's check."

"And then what?"

"Somehow when I started to write the name Malcolm Beckley I didn't feel right. The pen didn't want to write

69

Malcolm Beckley. My hand was stiff and the signature didn't look like the signature on the check, even I could tell that."

"What happened?"

"I guess the girls who run the cashier counters there get accustomed to cashing traveler's checks for guys who are pretty nervous. I know some fellow who was standing at the next window was having trouble with a personal check, but with a traveler's check they just didn't seem to pay too much attention. The girl looked at it, flipped it over, then looked at me and asked if she could see some identification.

"I produced my driving license, she looked at it, checked the description, made a little notation on the back of the check and handed me out the money."

"What did you do?"

"I was beginning to have the damnedest feeling, like I was whirling around in space somehow. I went over to a roulette table and turned the money into chips and started putting the chips on the numbers like mad."

"Then what?"

"My God," he said, "did I get lucky! I guess I must have been completely crazy. I put the whole stack of chips on the red, and the red came up. I let it lay, and the red came up again. I still let it lay, and the red came up the third time. Then I scraped the chips all in and put a big stack on number twenty-six, and twenty-six came. I made a couple of bum guesses on numbers, then put a big stack of chips on the red, and the red came again, and I let it lay, and the red came again, and I scooped up the whole pile of chips and all of a sudden while I was doing it, memory came back to me just as though someone had jerked a curtain from in front of my eyes."

"What happened?"

"I just collapsed on a stool and I remember somebody asking me if I wasn't feeling good. A house man came up and took charge of me and pushed away a couple of guys who probably were intending to roll me. He took me over to the cashier's window and cashed in my chips. I had over eighteen hundred dollars.

"I'll say one thing for these places, they sure run them on the square. This house man told me, 'You're not feeling good, and if you'll take my advice you'll go home and go to bed. We'll be glad to have you come back whenever you're feeling good and we'll give you some action on that money. You can take it away from us if you're lucky, and we'll take it away from you if you aren't lucky, but right now we'd like to have you home and in bed.'"

"What did you do?"

"I got in the car. I knew right where I'd parked it. I remembered the whole damned thing. I could remember everything just as plain as day, just the way I'm telling it to you now. I came out here to this motel and I've been here ever since. I go across the street to the restaurant and eat there. I'm afraid to go uptown. I'm afraid to appear in public. I'm afraid to communicate with anyone. I know that I should have gone to the police the minute I recovered my memory, but having cashed that traveler's check—well, that's where I burned my bridges. I'm stuck now.

"If I can get past the age of thirty-five without being picked up for a crime I'm okay, but there's a damned self-righteous guy who has all of my money tied up who would just love to jerk the rug out from under me, and if I'm picked up for a major crime, you can bet that's what's going to happen.

"I made up my mind I'd stay here just as long as I could, right here in one place. They think at the motel that I'm waiting for the six-week residential qualification so I can get a divorce—they don't ask questions in this town, and believe me, I'm not volunteering any information."

I said, "You're wrong about one thing."

"What?"

"It isn't being picked up for any crime before you're thirty-five that breaks the trust," I said. "It's being *convicted* of a major crime."

71

"Well, what's the difference?"

"One hell of a lot of difference," I said. "If you sit tight, if you don't co-operate, if you don't waive extradition, if you don't do one damned thing, if you get the best lawyer you can get and stall as much as you can, you stand a good chance of beating it out on the time limit."

"And then what?" he asked.

"Then," I said, "after you're thirty-five, the trustee has to turn the balance of the principal over to you, provided you haven't been *convicted* of a major crime."

"And then?"

"Hell!" I said, "Then you've got money, you can start really fighting."

"And until that time," he said, "I haven't got a dime that really belongs to me—but why are you talking this way? Aren't you connected with the police?"

I shook my head.

"You said you were an insurance investigator."

"I'm a private detective," I said. "Among other things, I was trying to find you. Do you know Sandra Eden?"

"Do I know her?" he said, his eyes lighting up. "How is she? How's Eleanore?"

"Fine," I said. "They're worried about you and they're flat broke."

He put his head in his hands. "I've thought about them dozens of times. I'd like to communicate with them but I don't dare. I just haven't know what to do. I know they need money. I'll have to get some in their hands somehow."

"All right," I said. "You can remember now pretty much what happened. The story that you've told to me."

"That's right."

"Now," I said, "we've got to retrace your steps. About where do you think you were when you recovered consciousness and jumped in the car and drove away?"

"I was on a dirt road," he said. "It was in the mountains. There was pine timber and there was a stream somewhere near by. I can remember the sound of rushing water. I know that I wanted to go over to the water and put my head in it and yet there was something that kept me from doing it, some kind of an unconscious fear that made me just want to get away from there as fast as I could—I don't think I've ever been as frightened in my life. . . . Say, what's your name?"

"My name," I told him, "is Donald Lam. Now, let's get back to this place where you were with the car. How far do you think you were from pavement?"

"About two miles."

"What kind of dirt road?"

"It was rough and rutted and, as I say, it was in the mountains. There was the feeling in the air of elevation and there were pine trees but it was night. All I could see was what the headlights showed."

"And when you hit the paved road you turned *up* a grade?"

"That's right, up a grade."

"And then what?"

"I drove, I guess for . . . oh, I don't know . . . maybe twenty miles."

"Now think carefully," I said. "When did you buy gas?"

"Not for quite a while."

"You looked at the gas gauge?"

"Yes. The tank was almost full."

"When you came to pavement," I said, "you turned uphill and you kept on going uphill for how long?"

"Well, it was uphill for a ways and then it was downhill and then I was winding around over sort of a plateau and then I went a long ways downhill. But remember, I turned off on this graveled road. Then it was daylight. I drove a long ways in mountains. Then there was farming land and I saw a sign that said Reno. I think it said Reno, forty miles."

"How far had you driven before you came to that sign?"

"I don't know. I would say . . . well, it was for hours. That part of the thing is still pretty mixed up. But I drove nearly all that day."

"Did you get the tank filled?"

73

"I think twice. I'm sure I got it filled twice, but it could have been three times. I was woozy."

"You didn't ask a service station man where you were or anything about it?"

"No, I just got gas and paid for the gas with cash and was on my way. You just can't understand those things, Lam. You probably have had the experience of waking up in the morning after you've had a sound sleep and wondering where you are. You are wide awake, you know everything about being awake except where you are. You can't remember for the life of you where you are. Then something happens and recollection comes back with a flood—well, that's the way it was with me. I knew that my memory was gone and I kept thinking it would come back and I just didn't want to do anything until it came back except keep on driving the car. I was nervous and jittery and I was hurt."

"You had blood on your face?"

"I had blood on my face and on my coat. I wiped most of it off."

"And when you got to the service station . . ."

"I stopped at a restaurant first, remember? I stopped and got something there, some coffee, and went into the rest room and locked myself in and looked at myself in the mirror and wet some paper towels and got the blood off. My head was sore—it's still sore."

"How much blood on your suit?" I asked.

He went over to a coat hanger, took down his coat and showed it to me.

"I washed out what I could," he said, "but you can still see some stains there."

"What did you wash it out with?"

"Cold water. I let it soak and washed out everything I could."

I said, "That's one hell of a story."

He looked at me dejectedly. "Ain't it?" he agreed.

"All right," I told him, "we go get some breakfast."

"And then what?"

"Then," I said, "I leave you right here just the way I found you until I do some more checking."

"What sort of checking?"

I looked him right in the eyes. "I want to find out what it was you were so damned afraid of," I said. "I want to find out why your instinct was that you had to leave that place just as fast as you could get in the car and scramble away."

He tried to meet my gaze but he couldn't. His eyes shifted and he shuddered.

"No ideas?" I prompted.

"No ideas I want to talk about," he said.

"All right," I told him, "let's go get some breakfast. You need coffee and you need a shave. I suppose you know no jury will ever believe your story."

"I know," he said.

6

I DROVE TO THE RENO AIRPORT, CAUGHT A plane which stopped at Sacramento, and at Sacramento picked up a plane for Bakersfield. In Bakersfield I rented a car and drove back up into the mountains. I kept looking for side roads.

The car rental agency was charging me by the mile, and every time the speedometer turned up another ten miles I thought of Bertha's face when she saw the expense account.

I never knew there were so many dirt roads leading down into little valleys. I tried every one I came to that seemed to fit the description, after I had passed over the summit.

Then when I was about ready to give up, I found it, a dirt road which went past an old weather-beaten cabin on down to a flat, and there was a stream brawling along in a pine-studded canyon.

There was a peculiar taint in the air. I walked downstream and learned nothing. I walked upstream and the air became odoriferous.

Five minutes later I had found him—or what was left of him. It wasn't a pretty sight.

I looked around very superficially, then got in my car, drove to the highway, went back to Bakersfield and walked into the sheriff's office.

The undersheriff was in charge of the place at the moment. I showed him my credentials.

"I want to report finding a body," I said.

"Where?"

I told him.

He wanted more details and I drew him a map.

"How did you happen to find it?" he asked.

"By a process of elimination," I said.

"Go ahead."

I said, "If you'll check with the California Highway Patrol you'll find that they've been looking for this man along this road for some time. They've been asked to make a careful search for any place where a car might have driven off the road.

"I'm not sure who this man is, but I think you'll find he's Malcolm G. Beckley, who picked up two hitchhikers and was on his way to Los Angeles when he simply disappeared."

"What about the car?" the undersheriff asked.

"No sign of the car near there that I could find. I didn't want to mess things up any."

The undersheriff thought things over for a moment, then said, "You could have reported this, you know, in a dozen different places. You came through towns where we have deputies and—"

"I wanted to report to headquarters," I said.

"Why?" he asked.

"Because I'm interested," I told him, "and I don't want the thing fouled up by having some country amateur get hold of it. I want an investigation right out of headquarters."

That made him feel a little better. He said, "You think this is a hitchhiker murder, huh?"

I said, "I don't know what it is. All I know is that Malcolm G. Beckley was going to drive most of the night to get to Los Angeles. He phoned his wife that he'd picked up a male hitchhiker and then later on that he'd picked up a blonde."

"What was the description of the blonde?" the undersheriff asked.

"Well stacked," I said.

"That's a hell of a description."

"It's only one the wife has," I told him. "It may not convey a picture to your mind but it does to mine."

He grinned at me and said, "Okay, Lam, let's go. If it's as hot as you think it is, we probably should make a good job of it. I'll go along myself and we'll have to pick up a local deputy in order to maintain protocol in the office."

"Okay by me," I told him. "Pick up anyone you want. Only let's get some good photographs before the place gets trampled all to hell, and let's be absolutely certain we get a positive identification."

"Insurance?" he asked.

"A hundred and fifty thousand dollars' worth," I told him.

He whistled.

"The guy had a sales business," I said. "It was a good business. He did things on a big scale."

"What about his wife?" the undersheriff asked.

"She's practical," I said. "I think she had given up hope of ever finding him alive when she called on me. If she could have found him alive, she didn't want him."

"What does she look like?" the undersheriff asked. "I mean, how old? What kind of a woman?"

"Twenty-six or twenty-seven," I said, "and full of curves in the right places."

He grinned. "Blonde?"

"Brunette."

"Practical?"

"Very. She knows that her husband was either bumped

77

off or that he ran off with the blonde. In either event she wants evidence. If he had been bumped off, she wanted a corpse before it got too badly decomposed to be identified. If he had run off with the blonde, she wanted evidence before the romance became so badly decomposed it couldn't be proved in a divorce court."

"She won't have hysterics, then," he said. "Think we could take her along?"

"It might be not so good until we have the guy's fingerprints."

"It may be a job getting those," he said.

"I've seen some expert work along those lines," I said. "You can inject liquid into the balls of the fingers with a hypodermic and then take prints."

"I know," he said. "We've got a good man here. He's up on the latest stuff. Let's go."

We drove back up into the mountains. By that time it was dark, but I was getting so I knew every foot of the road. We picked up a deputy in one of the larger cities before we passed over the summit and started down the grade on the other side. We also picked up a deputy coroner.

It was one messy job.

We didn't need any post-mortem to tell us that it was murder. The back of the guy's head had been smashed in, and the murder weapon was lying right there on the ground, a jack handle about two feet long. The whole top of the guy's skull was like a smashed eggshell.

There was one strange thing about the case. That was a hat that was presumably the dead man's hat. It was fifty feet away from the corpse.

I suggested to the undersheriff that it would be a good plan to measure the exact distance and show it in a photograph.

He looked at me superciliously. "What's the idea, Lam? It's windy up and down this canyon. The man's hat blew along the ground until it fetched up against that clump of sagebrush and that's where it happens to be today. Maybe next week it would be somewhere else."

"Perhaps some smart defense lawyer will want to know where it was today," I said. "Remember *you're* going to be the one who is on the witness stand. You're the one who will be cross-examined. With a hundred and fifty thousand bucks in insurance it may be quite a case."

He thought things over and said, "What the hell does the hat have to do with it, anyway?"

"Take a good look at it," I said.

He looked at me instead and said, "Give."

"The hat," I said, "is in perfect shape. The guy had his hat off when the murderer brought the jack handle down on his skull."

"Well?" the undersheriff asked.

"Do you," I asked, "drive a car with a hat on or with it off?"

"Sometimes it's on and sometimes it's off," he said. "That doesn't prove a damned thing."

"Where do you keep your jack?" I asked.

"In the trunk. Why?"

I said, "If it should turn out that's the jack handle which fits the jack in Malcolm Beckley's car, it could make quite a difference. Remember the blond hitchhiker telephoned that he'd had a flat tire, that she'd hitchhiked in to get a repair car and send it back."

"But there wasn't any repair car," the undersheriff said. "At least that's what you told me."

I said dryly, "No one *remembers* being called by the blond hitchhiker around daylight in the morning."

He looked at me a minute, then went over and said to the deputy sheriff, "All right, Bill, let's get a tape measure and measure the distance of the hat from the body. Use plenty of flashlights. Take photographs showing the whole scene just the way we've found it. Get lots of pictures. This is going to be one hell of a case."

While they were working I kept prowling around. After a while I said, "Take a look over here, boys. It looks like someone became very ill and upchucked."

They came over with their spotlights, but they didn't pay much attention. "Sure," the undersheriff said, "they do

79

that lots of times. A guy will go through with a very bloody murder and then he'll have a reaction. It doesn't mean a thing."

"In my book," I told him, "every clue in a murder case means something."

His lips were smiling, but his eyes were cold. "I know, Lam," he said, "but this isn't your book. It's mine—remember?"

I remembered and told him so.

7

THEY FINALLY GOT THE BODY IN A PLASTIC sack and got it in an ambulance.

"Now what?" I asked Harvey Clover, the undersheriff.

"Now," he said, "we check fingerprints and we put out an all-points bulletin for Beckley's car. That should have been done a long time ago. Why didn't you think of it?"

"I thought of it."

"Why didn't you do it?"

"Because I wasn't told to."

"You weren't told to go out here and find the body, were you?"

"In a way."

"What are you getting at?"

I said, "Let's suppose Malcolm Beckley had taken off with that blond hitchhiker. Suppose they were holed up someplace. The authorities put out an all-points bulletin on his car. They're driving along the road and an officer flags them into the curb. He asks to see Beckley's driving license and tells him his wife has put out an alarm that his car was stolen. Beckley says his wife can go jump in the lake, that he's on business and he's tired of ringing her up and having her nag at him, that the blonde who is with him is not the hitchhiker he picked up day before yesterday, or last week, or whenever it was, but a brand new babe who was walking along the highway and he took pity on her. She's been with him no more than an hour, that when he called his wife on the fifth there wasn't any blond hitchhiker, that this was just one of those husband-and-wife jokes."

"I see your point," Clover said.

"Now let's make another point," I told him.

"What?"

"A woman telephoned Mrs. Beckley that there'd been a breakdown, that she was getting a repair car to go back from Rommelly and fix up the spare tire so Beckley could go on home. She wasn't going back, she was going to keep on hitchhiking."

"But," Clover said, "you tell me that no request for a repair car was ever made."

"That isn't what I said. I said that neither one of the places that send out tow cars could *remember* the call."

"What have you got in mind?" he asked.

I said, "If the woman was lying, if there hadn't been any flat tire, then the woman who called, whoever she was, was telling a lie. If she was telling a lie, she's probably mixed up in the murder. If she's mixed up in the murder, that leaves the man hitchhiker in the clear."

"Not necessarily," Clover said. "They could have worked it out between them."

"They *could* have," I said.

"All right. What's the idea?"

I said, "You have a polygraph man in your office, don't you?"

"Yes. Why?"

"Tonight," I said, "and before this gets out, let's go down to those garages and run those two guys on a lie detector."

His eyes narrowed.

"In that way," I said, "if one of them is lying, we can give the blonde a clear bill of health. Beckley was left back there on the road with a flat tire and a hitchhiker. The trunk was open, the jack was out, and the hitchhiker

81

was holding the jack handle. That is, he could have been holding it."

"And then the tire got fixed some way," Clover said.

"Sure, it got fixed. Somebody came along who had a pump. What would you do if you had a pump and you found a car stalled by the road?"

"I'll bite."

"You'd stand by while they used the pump and inflated the spare tire. Then the spare tire would be inflated and they'd say, 'thank you.' You'd put the pump in your car and drive on. There's no reason why you should stand around with your hands in your pockets waiting for them to take the car off the jack, put the flat tire in the trunk and get started."

"You're right," he said. "I'll telephone in. You got a preference?"

"The younger guy," I said, "is at the Night & Day Garage. He's tattooed. He's probably been in the navy. He has pin-ups stuck to the walls around his cot. If a well-stacked blonde—"

"I get it," he said. "We'll get the lie detector."

He telephoned in for a man to come out with a polygraph and we stuck around waiting.

The polygraph expert arrived with his lie detector right after midnight, and we went over to the Night & Day Garage.

The young chap who kept the place at night was on duty. He wasn't in bed but was sitting in an easy chair that he'd nailed together out of an old wooden chair and a platform. It made a comfortable seat. He had a radio going.

He remembered me and shook hands. I introduced the undersheriff and the lie detector expert.

The undersheriff did the talking. "You remember back on the fifth?" he asked. "That is, the night of the fifth and the morning of the sixth. We're trying to trace a repair car call."

"Yes, sir."

"What's your name?"

"Tom Allen."

"You know anything about that call?"

"No, sir. I was talking with this gentleman here, the investigator. I told him I don't know a thing about it. I think there's some mistake, it didn't come in here—it may have come in at the other garage, but it sure didn't come in here."

"How do you know it didn't?"

"How do I know anything?" Allen said with a faint trace of defiance. "Hell's bells, man! There's a book there. I have to put down on the book every call that comes in. There's a speedometer on the repair car and I have to account for every mile that car is operated. We get a dollar a mile for some service calls, fifty cents a mile for others, and twenty-five cents on others."

"All right," Clover said. "Just answer questions. Keep a civil tongue in your head. Do you understand?"

"Yes, sir."

"All right. Sit down in that chair. Now, this man is a polygraph expert. You know what a polygraph is?"

"It's a lie detector?"

"That's right. It's a lie detector. We're going to run you on the lie detector and see whether you're telling the truth or not."

"I don't know as I'd like that."

"You mean you won't take a lie detector test?"

Allen looked down at the floor, moistened his lips with his tongue, said after a while, "I'm not refusing to take no lie detector test."

Clover motioned to the expert. "Go ahead," he said.

The lie detector man said, "The conditions aren't the best here. I can't guarantee that—"

"Go ahead," Clover said.

The lie detector man took over. "Now, look," he said. "The polygraph is a scientific instrument. It measures your blood pressure, it measures your skin sensitivity and resistance, it measures your respiration. When I finish giving you this lie detector test, I'll know absolutely whether you're telling the truth or not. Do you understand?"

Allen merely nodded.

"Roll up your sleeve," the expert said. "I'm going to put a pressure cuff on your arm so that we can get your pulse and run your blood pressure chart."

Allen rolled up his sleeve. He took a deep breath, then settled back in the chair. The polygraph expert adjusted his machine, took out half a dozen playing cards from his pocket. "See those?" he said.

Allen nodded.

"Think of one. Just *think* of it. Don't touch it, don't make a move. Just think hard about one card. Have you picked it?"

"Yes."

"All right," the lie detector man said. "I want you to lie to me now. I want to see what your pattern is when you lie."

"What do you mean?"

"I'll ask you whether the card you picked was the ace of spades. You say no. Even if it was the ace of spades, you say no. Don't say anything except no. Do you understand?"

"Uh-huh."

"Just say no. Even when I come to the right card, you lie to me. Say it wasn't the card."

"Okay."

The polygraph man adjusted the equipment, tested the pens, said, "Did you choose the ace of spades?"

Allen said, "No."

The expert waited five seconds, said, "Did you choose the queen of hearts?"

"No."

"Did you choose the ten of diamonds?"

"No."

"Did you choose the king of clubs?"

"No."

"Did you choose the four of hearts?"

"No."

"Did you choose the seven of spades?"

"No."

84

The examiner said, "All right. I'm going to run through the questions once more in the same order. You answer the same way. Do you understand?"

"Uh-huh."

"All right. Did you choose the ace of spades?"

Allen said, "No."

The expert went on through the whole list of cards. When he got done he said, "All right, Tom. I think I understand your psychological reactions now."

"What do you mean?"

The expert said, "You chose the four of hearts."

Allen looked startled.

"Now," the polygraph man said, "we'll go back to the evening of the fifth and the morning of the sixth—we'll start talking about the morning of the sixth. Do you understand?"

"Uh-huh."

The clockwork mechanism of the lie detector was moving along. The ruled paper was revolving slowly over the drums and the needles were pulsating with the changes in Allen's blood pressure, his pulse, his respiration and the skin sensitivity. The expert adjusted his needles once more.

"Is your name Tom Allen?"

"Yes."

The needle on the blood pressure indicator moved upwards, kept moving upwards for a few seconds, then moved back.

"Have you had dinner tonight?"

"Yes." The needle moved along regularly.

"Did you have a call from a blond woman early on the morning of the sixth?"

"No."

"Do you smoke?"

"Yes."

"Did any woman ring the night bell and ask you to go down the road to a car that had a flat tire?"

"No."

"Do you ever play poker for money?"

"Yes."

85

"Do you ever cheat?"

"No."

"Have you ever cheated?"

"No."

"Are you married?"

"No."

"Have you been in the navy?"

"Yes."

"Did you answer any call on the morning of the sixth and go out to repair a flat tire?"

"No."

"Now, just a minute," the lie detector expert said, "I'm going to run you through once more, Tom. I'm going to ask the questions in the same order. They'll be the same questions."

Tom Allen sat there, saying nothing.

"You understand?"

"I understand."

The polygraph man went through the same questions again. Then he released the pressure cuff, took off the harness around Tom Allen's chest and said, "I'm sorry, Tom, but you can't get by with it."

"What do you mean?"

"You're lying."

"The hell I am."

"All right, I'll show you," the expert said. "I asked you this question about the blonde. Notice what happened to your blood pressure. I asked you about the call on the morning of the sixth. Notice the same thing with your blood pressure. Notice your breathing up here. See that little catch in your respiration? Now, I'll tell you something else. Tom Allen isn't your real name.

"Now then, Tom, you're in a bind. This isn't just playing around. This is murder. You've been lying. You've suppressed material evidence. You're going under an assumed name. You've been in the navy. We're going to take your fingerprints. Within twenty-four hours we'll have your complete history."

Allen slumped down lower in the chair.

"Ever been in trouble?" Clover asked, taking over.

Allen didn't answer the question for a minute.

"Okay," Clover said, "I guess we'll take you along with us. You're a material witness and we'll check your record. This is a murder rap. It could be pretty bad."

"Hell!" Tom Allen said, "I ain't mixed up in any murder. Sure, I've been in trouble. I did a stretch in Nevada. I was on parole and I jumped parole. So what? That doesn't make me guilty of any murder."

"What about that call on the morning of the sixth?" Clover asked.

"All right," Allen said. "I'll tell you the truth. I was sleeping and I sleep pretty sound, see? The bell rang a couple of times and I got up and fumbled around for my pants and turned on the light and went to the door. I was just pulling my pants on. I opened the door expecting to see some guy standing there and here was this babe—and was she a knockout!

"Okay, she told me there was a car down the road that was in trouble, that the fellow had had a puncture and the spare tire was flat and he didn't have any pump and could I go down and fix it."

"What did you do?"

"She moved on in through the doorway while she was talking. I asked her who she was and she said she was just a hitchhiker, that who she was didn't make any difference, that the man had the car and he had money enough to pay for the service.

"Well, I told her there wasn't too big a hurry and I was going to make a little coffee before I went down there and would she join me in a cup?

"She said she would.

"So, I took her back here and turned on the electric plate under the coffee percolater and . . . well, one thing led to another and after a while it was too damned late to go down there and get that fellow with the spare tire. I figured he'd either sent some other message that had gone to the other garage or that he'd managed to get his flat tire fixed and was long gone."

87

"What happened to the blonde?" Colver asked.

"She kidded around with me for a while and finally told me she had to be on her way, that she was hitchhiking—boy, was she a dish! She was a peroxide blonde with sort of bluish eyes, not just straight blue but a darkish blue—and the smoothest skin!"

"Find out who she was?"

"I sure as hell tried," Allen said. "Boy, I'd like to have had her phone number, and I'd sure like to meet up with that dame again! But she was smart. Every time I'd ask her a question about where she came from or where she was going or anything she'd just make some smart crack, and then I'd try to question her and she'd lead me off on some kind of a detour and the first thing I'd know I was stranded out someplace and she was laughing at me."

"It seems to have been a pretty easy pickup for you," Clover said.

"That's what you think," Allen said. "I'm telling you, she wanted the coffee when she came in. She wasn't afraid of me, she wasn't afraid of anything. She was a girl who could make her own way. She'd been making her own way.

"I found out this much about her. She'd been slinging hash around the country. She said she could always get a job when she wanted to stop but she was restless. She didn't want to stop—boy, a babe like that *could* be restless, too! She had what it takes. She could get by anywhere.

"And she wasn't anybody's dish, don't get that idea through your head. I've known lots of women. I can tell. She was lonely and she wanted some coffee and . . . well, she liked me. I knew the minute I opened the door and she was looking at me that she liked me."

"And that gave you ideas?" Clover asked.

"That gave me ideas," Allen said. "There's some people that you don't click with and they don't click with you and there's some people the minute you see them, you click. Well, that's the way it was with this babe. We clicked."

"And you've denied ever having received a call?"

"Sure I have. What did I want to do, get myself fired?"

"Where did this woman go?"

"She said she was going toward Los Angeles, I know that. That's all I know. She didn't leave here until nearly seven o'clock. She wasn't in any great hurry. The day man comes on at seven-thirty, and if it hadn't been for that she'd have waited until noon."

"You know you can get in a hell of a lot of trouble over this," Clover said.

"What do you mean—can get?" Allen said. "I am . . . I hadn't expected that question about whether my name was Tom Allen. I know I jumped about a foot on that one—now the parole board in Nevada will get me and they'll throw the book at me. I'm right back in the prison at Carson City. I promised the warden there I'd go straight and never be back. He doesn't like guys who don't keep their promises. I'm in bad."

"Okay, you're in bad," the undersheriff said. "First, however, you're going in with us as a material witness. . . . Now, you'd know this blonde if you saw her again?"

"Would I know her! Boy, oh, boy, would I know her!"

Clover looked at me and said, "Well, that puts it right square on the shoulders of the other hitchhiker, the man who was left behind."

I said, "I thought this guy was lying when I talked with him."

"You and your smart cracks!" Allen said. "Hell, I had the wool pulled over your eyes from the time I first talked with you. You fell for my story hook, line and sinker."

"Then why did I come back with the law?" I asked.

"By God, I'd like to know the answer to that one!" Allen said. "I knew I was licked when you showed up with the law. I knew I was licked one way or the other. Hell's bells, I've got five years dangling from the end of my fingers; any time you take my fingerprints, I'm hooked."

Clover looked at me with grudging gratitude. "You know," he said, "we don't ordinarily cotton to private dicks from Los Angeles, but I owe you one on this, Lam. You had a right hunch."

"Thanks," I said. "Maybe you can do something for me sometime."

"You call on me and I'll do it," Clover said.

He turned to Tom Allen. "Okay, Tom. Get your things together. Ring up your boss. Tell him he's going to have to get somebody else to keep the place open tonight. You're headed for another bed and you can't take all those pinups with you."

8

I GAVE HARVEY CLOVER A DESCRIPTION OF the Roadracer car. He wrote down the license number, then telephoned in to have an all-points bulletin put out on the car.

"What's next?" I asked.

"Back to Bakersfield," he said.

"Any more work to be done up here?"

He shook his head.

"What do we do with Tom Allen?"

"He goes back to Bakersfield, we notify the Nevada authorities and see if they want him. We don't really have anything on him here."

I said, "I'd like to play a hunch."

"What's that?"

"Back at Central Creek there's a restaurant. A blond waitress is working there. She started work on the sixth. I'm just wondering if she could fit into the picture."

"That's a long ways to go on a hunch," Clover said.

"I know it is, but we could take Tom Allen down there and see if he could make an identification."

Clover thought it over.

I said, "It would be a shame to have a material witness in our hands and then let her slip through our fingers."

That did it. He said, "Okay, let's go. We'll take Allen with us."

"What about the other people?"

"We'll let them get some sleep. This polygraph expert was up a good part of last night. He can roll in at a motel and get some sleep while we're making the trip."

The three of us, Clover, Tom Allen and I, made the trip down the mountain to Central Creek.

By that time Tom Allen had decided he was hooked and had clammed up. He wasn't talking. Clover was tired, and for the most part we made the trip in silence.

A mile from Central Creek Clover slowed the car. "Let me handle this my way," he said.

"You're handling it," I told him.

Clover turned to Tom Allen. "Know why we took you down here?" he asked.

"No idea in the world," Allen said. "You're driving. I'm riding."

Clover pulled up in front of the café and stopped. "Let's get some coffee," he said.

"You taking me right through to Nevada?" Allen asked.

"I'm driving," Clover said. "Remember?"

"Yeah, I remember," Allen said sullenly.

The three of us walked into the restaurant. The blond waitress was behind the counter. She looked up as we came in. She recognized me, smiled, looked at Tom Allen and her face showed a quick spasm of expression. Then Allen made some sign and her face became a mask.

I looked at Clover. His face showed no expression.

We went up to the counter and sat down.

The waitress said, "Hello," to me, "you must get around."

"I do," I agreed.

She put out three glasses of water. For a moment her eyes met those of Tom Allen.

"Ham and eggs," Clover said. "What do you boys want?"

Allen said, "What do you do with a prisoner. Do you—?"

"Shut up," Clover said. "Do you want ham and eggs?"

"Yes."

The waitress looked at me. I nodded. "Ham and eggs."

"Three ham and, Pops," she called through the window. "How do you want them? Straight up or easy over?"

"Straight up," Clover said.

"Easy. Very, very easy over," Allen said.

"Straight up," I said.

She relayed the orders.

"Coffee," Clover said.

She put out three coffees.

"Ever seen this man before?" Clover asked her.

She looked at me and said, "Sure. He was in here—"

"Not him—this one." Clover jerked his thumb toward Tom Allen.

The waitress looked him over leisurely, slowly shook her head.

"This the one?" Clover asked Allen.

Allen shook his head positively. "Never saw her before in my life."

Clover showed his star. "What's your name?"

"Edith Jordan. Why? Does it make any difference?"

"It may. How long you been here?"

"Morning of the sixth."

"What time?"

"Around ten o'clock, I guess. . . . Anything else?"

"Not now."

She turned away, her shoulders stiff with hostility.

Clover sighed. "Well, at least we've had the ride."

Clover was tired and showed it. He put his elbow on the counter, his head in his hand, and closed his eyes.

I half turned my back so I wasn't watching Allen, but there was a mirror in the back which enabled me to keep an eye on him.

I looked for him to make some signal.

He didn't make any signal. The waitress didn't seem inclined to conversation and none of us said anything.

Pops put out the ham and eggs. We ate, had refills on the coffee. Clover looked at me and raised his eyebrows. I nodded and said to the waitress, "I'll take the check."

I paid the check and left her a dollar tip. We went back to the automobile.

"Want me to spell you?" I asked Clover.

"I sure as hell do," he said, "but it's a county car and I'm responsible."

"I'll drive," Allen said, "and guarantee to get you there. That's one thing I can do—drive a car."

Clover said, "Nothing doing," and looked at me inquiringly.

"I can make it all right," I told him. "At least part way."

"Okay," he said. "Keep Allen up front with you. I'll be in the back seat. Don't try anything funny, Allen, or you'll arrive feet first."

"Hell!" Allen said. "What do you take me for—a damn fool? I know when I'm licked."

I got behind the wheel and drove the car. A couple of times I tried to get Allen in conversation. He wasn't having any.

We got back to Rommelly.

"Now what?" I asked Clover.

Clover got up from the back seat and pretended he hadn't been asleep. He stretched surreptitiously, yawned, looked around him, said, "We get our polygraph man and beat it back. It's a shame to wake him up. He's probably sawing it off."

He was in a motel. We went in and got him out of bed.

While we were waiting for the polygraph man to dress, Clover said to me, "Well, you're entitled to one bad guess. For the rest you've done all right."

"What do you mean, a bad guess?" I asked.

He jerked his head in the direction of Central Creek.

"What did you expect to prove, going in that way?" I asked.

"I was watching the girl," he said. "She looked us over and then her eyes shifted to you. If she'd known Allen,

93

particularly if she'd been the one who had been hitchhiking, she'd have shown some signs of panic."

"Think so?" I asked.

"Uh-huh," he said. "I've been with this business a long time."

I jerked my thumb toward the polygraph which was in a case. "Put that on Tom Allen," I said, "and ask him if he knows the waitress down there."

"Now, wait a minute," Allen said. "I've cooperated with you guys. I'm not going to give you any more cooperation."

"See what I mean?" I said to the undersheriff.

Clover looked at Allen thoughtfully, then looked at the polygraph expert. "Hook him up," he said.

"I'm not answering any more questions," Allen said.

"Hook him up," Clover said.

They put Allen in a chair and hooked him up on the polygraph.

"Have you eaten since I saw you last?" the expert asked.

Allen kept quiet.

"Is your name Tom Allen?"

There was no answer.

"Were you in Central Creek a short time ago?"

There was still no answer.

"Did you see anyone you knew in Central Creek?"

Again there was no answer.

"The name is Edith Jordan," I said.

"Do you know an Edith Jordan?"

Allen kept sullenly silent.

The polygraph expert looked at the chart, then looked up at Clover and nodded his head.

Clover cursed underneath his breath.

The polygraph expert said, "Allen, you're lying. Look here. Look at this curve. That's your blood pressure. That's your pulse. Look at your respiration. You know Edith Jordan. You've known her well. Take a look at this. Take a look at your own reactions when I asked the question."

Tom Allen kept his eyes straight ahead. He wouldn't even look at the chart which the polygraph expert thrust in front of him.

"Well?" Clover asked. "What's the answer, Allen?"

"No comment," Allen said. "I'm not talking to you guys."

"Your blood pressure is talking. Your reactions are talking," the polygraph expert said. "You've seen this girl before. You've known her well."

Allen started pulling off the straps which fastened the polygraph to him.

"The hell with you guys!" he said. "A man doesn't need to be a witness against himself. I know that much law."

"Tell it to the Nevada authorities when you go back," Clover said.

"I will," Allen said.

Clover went over to the phone, picked it up and put through a call for his deputy in Carver City. When he had him on the line he said, "Get in a car. Go over to the restaurant in Central Creek. It's a café. There's a blonde named Edith Jordan working there as a waitress. Pick her up and then telephone me. I'm here at the Summit Motel at Rommelly, Unit 26. Call me just as soon as you have her. . . . Hell, just pick her up, that's all. . . . All right, tell her it's on suspicion of murder. . . . That's right, that's what I said, murder."

Clover slammed up the phone and glared at Tom Allen. "Now," he said, "you're in this right up to your neck."

Allen said nothing, but sat sullenly silent.

"All right," Clover said to the polygraph expert, "get your stuff packed. We'll get ready to start as soon as we get the call from Central Creek. We'll have the deputy bring that blonde up and we'll all go in together."

"If she's there," I said.

"What the hell do you mean, if she's there?" Clover asked.

"Nothing," I said.

We got the car all packed up, then went back to the motel and waited.

After a while the phone rang. Clover answered it, talked for a while, then said, "All right, put out a bulletin. Pick her up—suspicion of murder."

He slammed up the phone and turned to me. "Gone," he said. "She left the place within five minutes after we did, hitchhiked a ride and we don't know in which direction."

"Well," I said, "as I've been told, a man is entitled to miss the bull's-eye once."

"Sonofabitch!" Clover said disgustedly. "And we had her right in our hands. . . . Damn it, Lam, why the hell didn't you tell me?"

"You said you wanted to play it your way."

"Well, you should have known—"

"Don't sell yourself short, Clover," I said. "It may be a pretty good way."

"What do you mean?"

"You can pick her up all right," I said. "Flight is evidence of guilt. You didn't have too much on her before, and if Allen wouldn't talk, you could have had some trouble. A lie detector test isn't evidence in the California courts. The way it is now you've got something you can use."

Clover thought that over, then grinned and said, "Damned if you haven't got something there, Lam. Come on, let's go."

We started the long ride back to Bakersfield.

The sun was hot by the time we pulled into the sheriff's office and there was a bulletin on the Roadracer car. It had been picked up in Bridgeport, California, parked by the side of the road abandoned, and it had evidently been gone over carefully by someone who wiped off all fingerprints. There wasn't a fingerprint on the car.

Clover turned from the telephone to relay the report to me.

"Ask them about the spare tire," I said.

"What about the spare tire?" Clover asked in the telephone. After a minute he turned to me and said, "Spare tire okay, all inflated."

"What about the jack handle?"

Again he relayed the question into the telephone and came back with the answer. "The jack is in the trunk but there's no jack handle. It's a hydraulic jack that takes an iron handle and they can't find the handle anywhere."

"But the spare tire is all inflated?"

"All inflated."

"Then he got it fixed *somewhere*," I said.

Clover's eyes narrowed. "How right you are, Lam. Thanks for the tip."

He whirled to Tom Allen. "You sonofabitch!" he said. "This blonde came to you and told you about the car that was in trouble down the road. It was only about ten miles away and the man was dough-heavy. You went down there with a repair car and the blonde went back with you. You fixed up the tire and then conked the guy over the head with the jack handle, took him off the road a couple of miles and dumped him."

"And what about the other hitchhiker?" Allen asked. "What did I do with him? Kill him, too, or was he in on the deal? Go on, send me back to Nevada."

"Send you back to Nevada, hell!" Clover said. "We're holding you right here on suspicion of murder until we can get this thing cleared up."

"Suits me," Allen said. "You can't hang a murder rap on me."

"I'll give you a damned good demonstration of a man trying," Clover said. "We don't like cons to start lying to us when we're investigating a murder case."

"I think I'm going to want an attorney," Allen said.

"What you're going to want is a damned good kick in the tail," Clover said angrily. "You passed that blond waitress some sign and she slipped right through our fingers."

"I never knew any blond waitress," Allen said.

Clover glared at him.

I looked over at Clover and said, "Got an airplane schedule here? I want the next plane to Los Angeles."

"We'll take you down to the airport," Clover said. "You've done all right, Lam."

"Despite my one bad hunch?" I asked.

"Forget it," he said, "and get the hell out of here before the newspaper reporters start talking to you."

"They'll talk with *me*," Tom Allen said.

"That's what *you* think," Clover told him. He turned to a deputy and said, "Bury this smart aleck sonofabitch."

Clover took an airlines folder from his desk, looked through the schedule, looked at his watch, said, "Come on, Lam. We've just got time to make the Los Angeles plane."

9

I HADN'T HAD SLEEP FOR SO LONG I HAD almost forgotten what it tasted like, but I went to the barbershop at the Los Angeles Airport and got a shave, a shampoo, a face massage, and came out feeling a little better.

Then I rang up the Beckley apartment.

Daphne Beckley's voice sounded fresh and rested, and without a trace of nervous tension.

"I think they found your husband," I said.

"With or without the blonde?"

"Without."

There was a silence. Then she said, "Are you trying to break something to me gently, Donald?"

"Yes."

"Don't do it. I like the direct approach."

I said, "You're a widow."

"When did it happen?"

"The night of the fifth or early on the morning of the sixth, as nearly as anyone can tell. Apparently one or the other of the hitchhikers, or perhaps both, murdered your husband, stole his car and took off."

"Want to come up and tell me about it?" she asked.

"I haven't had any sleep since—I've forgotten what a bed feels like."

"You poor boy," she said sympathetically. "Come up and let me give you some coffee. But I *must* hear the details, Donald. I . . . I'm not going to put on a scene. I have been expecting this ever since . . . well, before I called you in. I promise not to complicate the situation by nerves or tears but I do want to know what you've found out."

"I'll be up," I told her.

"I'll be waiting."

I took a cab up to the Ringold Apartments and went to 721.

Daphne Beckley opened the door almost as soon as my finger had pressed the mother-of-pearl button which sounded the muted chimes in the interior of the apartment.

She put her hand in mine as she opened the door and made no effort to withdraw it until after she had drawn me into the apartment and pushed the door closed behind us.

"Have the police been in touch with you?" I asked, when she had the door closed.

She shook her head.

"They will," I said. "Any minute now."

"Donald, what am I going to do?"

"What do you mean?"

"I don't want to be a hypocrite. I don't want to put on an act of great grief. As a matter of fact, Malcolm and I had been very affectionate when we were together, but he'd been philandering and I knew it, and . . . well, I wondered just how far it had gone, whether it was going to disrupt our marriage or not.

"I have often wondered how a woman would feel under these circumstances. Naturally, I feel that something has gone out of my life and I know that when the first shock wears off I'm going to be terribly lonely. I'm going to miss him. I'm going to miss hearing the phone ring and hearing his voice giving me those little code signals and messages that we used to have. But . . ."

She hesitated.

"But," I said, "you're young, you're attractive, you've got a swell figure and you're going to have a hundred and fifty thousand bucks."

"You mean that a new life is going to open up before me?"

"Something like that. It can, if you want it to."

She looked me straight in the eyes and said, "Donald, I want it to."

I nodded.

"But," she said, "people are going to think me terribly heartless if I don't sit and mope for several months. Donald, I just can't do that. I haven't got it in me to be that much of a hypocrite. I like life, I like laughter, I like lights at night, and I'm going to tell you the truth, Donald —I can't get along without a man in my life."

I nodded.

"Now then, Donald, tell me what I'm going to do."

I said, "When the police let you know that your husband's body has been identified, you're going to tell them that you are prepared for that information because I have already told you he was murdered. You're going to be dry-eyed but sort of numbed by the shock. You're going to cry at the funeral. You can't keep from crying. No matter how you have felt toward a man, when you see him at his funeral, you're going to cry. All women do."

She nodded.

"Then," I said, "you're going to travel. You're going to start out trying to forget. You're going to be a poor, crushed flower. You're going to get on a plane, you're going to tell everyone you're going to Europe, and, instead of that, you're going to go on a cruise ship to South America.

"On the cruise ship people will know you're a widow but they won't know *when* your husband died."

"Then what happens when I get back?"

"Why get back?" I asked.

"What do you mean?"

"What's holding you here?" I asked. "Relative, family, what?"

"A few friends."

"Friends of both of you?"

"You mean Malcolm's friends as well as mine?"

I nodded.

"That's right," she said. "Malcolm was terribly gregarious. He has a lot of friends, and—"

"And every one of them will want to live your life for you," I said. "Some of the men will be on the make. Some of the women will be intensely critical, no matter what you do. If you start mourning they'll say, 'Well, goodness sakes alive! You'd think that Daphne would snap out of it. She should be sensible. All the mourning and sniffling in the world isn't going to bring poor Malcolm back to life.' "

Her eyes narrowed thoughtfully.

"If, on the other hand," I said, "you start trying to pick up where you left off, you'll find that the whole thing is different. The friends you knew were married couples around your own age. Now you're a single woman, a widow, and, as such, a potential source of danger to the stability of any marriage. The wives will gradually draw away from you so their husbands won't be around you. You'll pick up a few unattached males, and if you try to play along with them, the talk will be, 'Well, for goodness sakes! You'd think Daphne Beckley would at least have the decency to wait until Malcolm had got cold in his grave before she started gallivanting around. Did you see the way she looked at that wavy-haired artist after she was dancing with him? You could see everything right in her eyes. I was never so disgusted in my life!' "

Daphne was thoughtfully silent for a long time. Then she said, "Donald, I think you're right. I'm so glad I came to the firm of Cool & Lam. You—"

The phone rang.

She looked at the phone with a frown, then said, "Do *you* think I'm so terribly attractive, Donald?"

"Sure, you are," I said. "I'll bet that of all the friends you have in the young married set, there isn't a woman you know who has your figure."

The phone kept ringing.

Daphne made an impatient gesture, got up and moved toward the phone. She picked it up, said, "Hello." Then after a moment, said, "Speaking."

She was silent for several seconds while the telephone made squawking noises, then she said, "I have already been advised of the situation. Mr. Donald Lam, a detective of the firm of Cool & Lam, has just finished reporting to me. . . . I'm rather upset at the moment. Would you mind if I took a little time to . . . to adjust myself. I . . . I prefer to talk it over later. . . . I know, but there's nothing I can say. I—Yes, I'll put Mr. Lam on the telephone."

She nodded to me and extended the phone.

I picked up the phone and a voice said, "This is Frank Malone of the *Tribune*. We're running a short article about Malcolm Beckley being murdered by a hitchhiker. What can you tell me about it?"

"Nothing without permission," I said.

"Well, can you get permission? We want a story. We hate to bother the widow, but we want to get the facts— we're not going to play it up too big, but he was a businessman and has a local background, and we want to carry the story."

"How much of a story?"

"Hell, Lam, I don't know. You don't know. It depends on what the facts are. It depends on what other news comes in, and how much cutting they do after I get it written."

I looked over at Daphne, put my hand over the mouthpiece and said, "How much do I tell them?"

"Anything you want," she said. "It's okay with me."

I said into the telephone, "Okay, here are the facts. Malcolm Beckley was driving back toward Los Angeles on the night of the fifth. He sent his wife a post card from Carver City. He picked up a hitchhiker in Carver City, and before he got to Central Creek, had picked up a woman hitchhiker—a well-stacked blonde. He called his wife from Central Creek.

"Some five hours later his wife received a phone call from a woman who was calling from Rommelly. She said Malcolm Beckley was stalled with a flat tire about ten miles out of town, and that she was sending a repair car back.

"Beckley never showed up.

"After a while, Mrs. Beckley got worried. She called the two garages in Rommelly and was told no call had been received.

"Yesterday the sheriff's office at Kern County made a detailed search of side roads and discovered a body, which I understand has now been identified as that of Malcolm Beckley. Someone had beaten in his head with the handle of a jack, presumably the jack from his own car.

"The car was recovered after an all-points bulletin had been put out. It was found near Bridgeport, parked by the side of the road, headed toward Nevada. Authorities believe it had not been there over twenty-four hours when it was discovered.

"The undersheriff at Bakersfield got a tip that one of the traveler's checks Beckley had been carrying at the time of his death was cashed in a Reno casino—those are the facts as I have them. I got my information from Harvey Clover, the undersheriff. He's a swell guy."

"What kind of a lead can you give me on this well-stacked blonde?" Malone asked. "That sounds like a real angle for a story."

"Well," I said, "I'd want you to get that story from the undersheriff at Bakersfield. I accompanied him to the Night & Day Garage in Rommelly. A man named Tom Allen was on duty nights. He said he'd never received a call from a blonde about a stalled car on the morning of the sixth. The undersheriff put him on a lie detector. That lie detector showed the guy was lying.

"Then Tom Allen confessed that along about five o'clock in the morning this curvaceous blonde had rung the night bell. She'd wanted him to send a repair car back ten miles down the road. He decided to make some coffee first and asked her to join him. She joined him in coffee, and by the time they finished drinking the coffee, they both decided it was too late to send a repair car back—either Beckley would have fixed things up and gone on, or he would have sent in a call to the other garage."

"That gives it an angle," Malone said enthusiastically. "We can play that up pretty big. It's a good idea—BLOND SIREN DETAINS REPAIRMAN WHILE LOCAL SALES EXECUTIVE MURDERED BY HITCHHIKER."

"Better be a little careful about that," I said.

"What do you mean?"

"How do you know it wasn't the blonde who murdered him?"

"She wouldn't have murdered him and then gone to a garage to have a repair car sent back."

"How do you know she wouldn't?"

"It stands to reason," he said. "The repair car would have found the murdered man, and the blonde would have been taken into custody for questioning."

"How do you know the repair car would have found him? The body wasn't where she said Beckley had a flat tire."

"Then the other hitchhiker must have driven the body off the road and dumped it."

"Could be," I said. "On the other hand, remember that the woman's call came through about five hours after Beckley had called his wife from Central Creek. That means he was only averaging about ten miles an hour—there's quite a time element there that wasn't accounted for."

"But what happened to the other hitchhiker?"

"Perhaps he was murdered, too," I said. "So far they've only found one body. We know this. Beckley told his wife the blond hitchhiker was in the back seat."

"Hot dog!" Malone said.

"Moreover," I went on, "Beckley apparently was clubbed to death with the jack handle out of his car. Therefore, somebody must have opened the trunk in order to get the jack handle. Now, why did they open the trunk?"

"That's easy. There was a flat tire. That's what the girl said."

"But," I said, "the car was recovered in Bridgeport and the spare tire was inflated and there was no evidence of a flat."

"It was murder all right?" Malone asked.

"Sure, it was murder. A guy wouldn't commit suicide by beating himself over the head with a jack handle. There are better ways."

The reporter thought that over. "Say," he said, "you're giving me a whale of a story! This may be worth going up to Bakersfield and getting some interviews and pictures."

"When you do that," I said, "you can look for a missing blonde from a café in Central Creek. The café is operated by Dorothy Lennox."

"What's the story about this blonde?"

"The undersheriff at Bakersfield will give it to you."

Malone's voice showed excitement. "Say," he said, "this is really getting into a story! How long did this babe and the repairman spend in the hay before—"

"Who said they were in the hay?"

"Well, they were sitting there—What the hell were they doing, drinking coffee?"

"How would I know?"

"What did this repairman say?"

"He lied."

"And then he confessed?"

"That's right. He confessed."

"And what did he say they were doing?"

"I don't think the authorities went into complete details on that—at least they hadn't when I left. They probably will before they get done. Incidentally, Allen is an ex-con who is traveling under an assumed name and is wanted for parole violation in Nevada."

"Hell's bells!" Malone exclaimed. "This thing is— Why, hell, we can make a *real* feature out of this thing. Here's sex, mystery and murder and— You say it was five hours from the time Beckley telephoned his wife before the woman called up from Rommelly?"

"That's right."

"Maybe she called up after she'd been playing around with this ex-con."

"Could be."

"Would that make a difference?"

"It would make quite a difference in the time element."

"And somebody cashed a check in Reno, a check that had been stolen from Beckley?"

"Right."

"Woman or man?"

"Man."

"Then that would mean a man hitchhiker did it," Malone said.

"Not necessarily. They might have divided things up fifty-fifty."

Malone thought that over, said, "Thanks a hell of a lot, Lam. You've given me a real story here."

"In case you're grateful," I said, "you can remember that the firm name is Cool & Lam, and we have offices in—"

"Don't be silly," he said. "I wasn't born yesterday. You've given me a break and I'm going to be grateful. You'll find a nice paragraph in the article that Donald Lam, the brainy detective who accompanied police when they found the body of Malcolm G. Beckley, gave an exclusive interview to the *Tribune* in which he said blah, blah, blah."

"Nice going," I told him.

"And I'm going to want to get follow-ups," he said.

"You can reach us at our office," I said. "Either I'll be there or my partner, Mrs. Cool, will be available."

"Thanks a lot, Donald," he said, and hung up.

Daphne Beckley was looking at me with troubled eyes. "Donald, you're making quite a story of this."

"I'm not," I said. "The newspapers are going to."

"But you've given them lots of material."

"You said to."

"You hadn't told me that, about this girl and the garageman necking around until it was too late for the repair car to go back."

"I haven't had a chance yet to tell you lots of things."

She moved over on the davenport and patted the cushions beside her.

"All right. Come over and tell me," she said.

I walked over to the chair and sat down.

She made a little expression of disappointment. "I thought you wanted to—Well, I'd like to have you—Do you always turn down invitations to sit beside a client?"

I crossed over and sat down beside her. She poured coffee. I drank the coffee and she asked, "What about the blonde in the restaurant who disappeared?"

"She *could* be the mysterious blond hitchhiker," I said. "She could have hitchhiked to Rommelly, put in the call to you, gone to the garage to get the repair car, and then, after a while, perhaps her conscience bothered her and she hitchhiked back in order to make sure that your husband wasn't still stalled out there in the road."

"And when she didn't find the car, then what?"

"Then she got off in Central Creek and went in for a cup of coffee. The woman who was running the restaurant asked her to go to work and she decided to do so."

"In that case, she would be innocent of the murder."

"Probably."

"You think it was the man hitchhiker who did it, Donald?"

"I don't know. I'm not certain."

"Malcolm told me the woman was in the back seat."

"I've emphasized that in telling the story," I said.

I finished the coffee and put the cup down.

"You poor boy," she said. "You're just dead for want of sleep."

"I'm tired, but not dead."

She suddenly put her arm around me and leaned back, pulling my head down against her.

Her finger tips moved gently along my forehead, down over my eyes, around the back of my neck. "You poor boy," she droned. "You need sleep. Don't you want to sleep here?"

I let my cheek nestle against her and said, "That was the newspaper reporter. You haven't heard from the police yet. They'll be here, and——"

"Here?" she asked.

"Of course," I said.

Abruptly she pushed me away. "Donald," she said, "you must go home and get some sleep."

"It's an idea," I admitted.

She was on her feet, smiling farewells. "But don't forget me," she said.

"I won't."

"You'll be back?"

"In case there are any new developments I'll be back, but we've completed the job we were hired for."

She thought that over for a moment or two, then said, "Yes, I suppose you have. But . . . I hate to think of my husband's murder going unavenged."

"The police will be working on that angle," I said.

"Yes, I suppose so."

She went to the door, hesitated a moment, looked at me and said, "I'm so glad that I got your firm. Tell me, Donald, will there be any trouble with the identification?"

"It'll probably depend on the extent of decomposition. I think they can still get prints from the fingers. At least enough to make an identification. Had your husband had any military service?"

"Yes."

"His fingerprints are on file then. I don't think there'll be any trouble about the insurance."

"Donald," she said, smiling and tender at the same time, "I'm going to make a pun that probably hundreds of women have made."

"What?"

"You're a lamb," she said, and put her face up to be kissed.

I kissed her and then she was all solicitude, getting the lipstick off my face, arranging my tie and stroking my hair with her finger tips. "You naughty boy," she said. "You must go now."

"Why naughty?"

"Kissing me like that," she said. And then she opened the corridor door and I was out in the corridor.

The door slowly closed.

10

I DROVE TO THE EDEN APARTMENT.

Sandra opened the door and gave me her hand. A moment later I heard Eleanore Eden's voice saying, "Who is it, Sandra?"

"Mr. Lam."

Sandra's mother came toward me. "Oh, Mr. Lam," she said, and her eyes filled with tears.

"What is it?" I asked.

"What you did over at the grocery store—you didn't need to do that. We're not . . . well, it's hard to tell you how we feel. It was *such* a bighearted, generous act and . . ."

Her voice choked up.

"Forget it," I said. "Have you heard anything from Amos Gage?"

"The most peculiar thing happened," she said, "and I don't know what to do about it."

"What?"

"A telegram came stating that a sum of money had been sent by Amos Jones by Western Union telegram. I was requested to go to the branch office and they asked me some questions about Amos Jones—fortunately I didn't tell them I didn't know any Amos Jones. I did tell them I thought there was something wrong with the spelling of the name, and they asked me if I had any idea how much money was being sent me, and I said perhaps thirty dollars, and the cashier smiled and said it was three hundred dollars; that identification had been waived but she'd like to see some personal identification."

"When did this happen?" I asked.

"Late yesterday evening."

"And then what?"

"They had a draft all made out in my favor for three hundred dollars, and I signed my name on the back of it, and they gave me three hundred dollars—Mr. Lam, that must have been Amos Gage, but—"

"Where was it sent from, do you know?"

"No, I—Wait a minute, I do, too. It was someplace over in the desert . . . Bishop, that's the name of the place."

"I see," I said noncommittally.

I took the picture from my pocket, the one of Daphne Beckley in the Bikini bathing suit and the man standing next to her. I showed it to Eleanore.

Eleanore gasped. "Who in the world is that woman? Why, Mr. Lam, she's practically—"

"Never mind that," I said. "Who's the man?"

"Why, that's Uncle Amos."

"Let me see," Sandra said, pushing forward. Her mother hastily put her hand over the half of the photograph showing Daphne Beckley.

"Why, Mother, it *is* Uncle Amos! I've never seen him in a bathing suit."

I gently took the photograph from Mrs. Eden.

"Can you tell me where you got that?" she asked, and there was hurt in her voice.

"Not right now."

"I . . . I wonder when it was taken."

"I think," I said, "it was some sort of a gag. There's no doubt about that being a picture of Amos Gage?"

"Heavens, no! That is . . . well, you know how pictures are, but—"

"Sure," I said. "Those things do happen, you know. Pictures sometimes give a wrong impression. I just wondered if you'd recognize it."

"Why, yes . . . I'm almost sure that's Amos Gage but I can't understand his being with a woman of that . . ."

"What woman?" Sandra asked, as her mother's voice trailed into silence.

"The woman in the picture, dear. She's wearing a very daring bathing suit."

"Can I see?"

Mrs. Eden hesitated for a moment, then nodded to me. "I guess there's no reason why she shouldn't see it if she wants to."

Sandra looked at the picture with thoughtful speculation. She said only, "Why, Mother, that's the kind of bathing suits they wear in Europe. Uncle Amos hasn't been in Europe, has he?"

"We don't know *where* he's been," Mrs. Eden said.

Sandra said thoughtfully, "I'm not so sure, Mother."

"What?"

"About it being Uncle Amos. There's something about the eyes—the eyes don't look like Uncle Amos."

Mrs. Eden examined the picture once more. Then she turned to me. "Is it Amos Gage?" she asked.

"Frankly," I said, "I don't know. I thought there was a certain resemblance so I thought I'd ask you."

"There's a very remarkable resemblance, all right," she said, "but . . . do you have any reason to believe that it's *not* Amos Gage?"

"Yes," I said. "There's some reason to believe that it's not Amos Gage. That is, not the Amos Gage you know."

She handed the photograph back to me with a sigh.

"I don't think he'd have his photograph taken with a woman like that," she said.

There was a moment of silence.

"What shall we do with the money, Mr. Lam?"

"Spend it," I said. "Spend a good deal of it right now

111

for the things you're going to need. I'd lay in a stock of groceries, things that will keep—canned goods, dried food and things like that—things that won't spoil. And get plenty of eggs and meat to see you through the next week, everything that you can use that won't spoil before you can use it."

"Why? Do you have any news of Uncle Amos?"

"In a way," I said, "but only in a way."

"Can you tell me what you mean by that?"

I said, "I'm afraid Uncle Amos is not going to be able to make his usual donation and I think he wanted you to have money ahead so you could take care of things without being in want."

"But why should I invest the money in food now?"

I said, "I don't know. It was just my idea. I think you'd better do it."

"When?"

"Now."

"But I don't see why, Mr. Lam."

I said, "Someone might get the idea that the money has been sent to you wrongfully and try to take it away. They might try to impound the money but they wouldn't impound groceries."

"Why should anyone want to impound the money?"

"Oh, you can't tell," I said. "It's an unusual situation and—well, if Uncle Amos had wanted it so the money could be traced, he'd have sent it under his own name, wouldn't he?"

"Yes, I guess so."

"Well then, why not take the hint he's trying to give you and invest the money?"

"But Amos wouldn't do anything wrong. There wouldn't be any—Why, he'd never think of getting possession of any money that there was any question about, and if he sent it to us, why then—"

"Sure, sure," I said. "He wouldn't send it to you unless it was absolutely all right. That's why I suggest that you spend it."

"But, Mr. Lam, if there's any question about it—any
112

question whatever—spending the money is the last thing I want to do. I want to have it so we can return it."

"Return it to whom?"

"Well, to . . . to Amos, if that's what we're supposed to do."

"Amos is trying to tell you that he wants you to invest that money in groceries."

She studied me thoughtfully. "Are you trying to tell me that you know what Uncle Amos had in mind?"

"I'm trying to tell you that I know what Uncle Amos must have had in mind."

"Then you must have seen him."

I said, "I came to you specifically to give you some advice. Put your things on, go out now and start shopping. Spend about a hundred dollars of the money. Get lots of canned goods, lots of staples, things that will keep, and get some meat and eggs. Then take the rest of the money and pay the hospital so you can go ahead with your operation. Do that today. Get started."

Eleanore Eden thought things over for a few seconds, then abruptly arose, said, "You want me to go shopping now?"

"Now. . . . Then go make the payment to the hospital."

Sandra came close to my chair. "Did you see Uncle Amos?" she asked. "Is he all right?"

I said, "There are some questions I can't answer, Sandra, but I *think* Uncle Amos is all right at the present time. However, there may be reasons why he can't get in touch with you right now."

"You mean business reasons?"

"In a way, yes."

"He's making some sort of a deal in mining properties and doesn't want people to know where he is?"

"Well now, I couldn't say for sure that that was the reason," I said, "but if I were you I wouldn't speculate on that. I don't think you need to worry right at the moment. But I would be sure you have things to eat in the house."

"And you'll keep in touch with us?" Eleanore asked.

113

"Oh, sure," I said. "And then, of course, you know where I am, and you can always get in touch with me. Only be sure you ask for me personally and if I'm not there don't leave your name or number with anyone else. Just don't talk with anyone unless I'm there. Do you understand?"

She nodded.

"Well," I said, stretching and yawning, "I'll be going. I've been doing a lot of work without much sleep."

"On this case?"

I laughed and said, "We have lots of cases."

"Mr. Lam, would it be all right if I should pay you with a part of this—"

"It would not be all right," I said. "Furthermore, you're to forget that you know anything about me or ever came to the agency. Just—"

"But I couldn't lie."

"Certainly not. No one's asked you to lie. Simply forget about it and don't say anything unless, of course, you should be questioned specifically. If you are questioned, you can say that you didn't employ us to do anything. You remember, *you* never were at the office. Sandra went to the office and tried to get the firm to interest itself in finding her Uncle Amos. My partner, Mrs. Cool, said that we couldn't have anything to do with it. You remember that, Sandra?"

She nodded.

"Therefore," I said, "anything that I've done is done as a friend, so if anyone asks you if you *hired* detectives, you can say truthfully that you didn't. You haven't hired anybody."

"But why be so mysterious? Why shouldn't we tell the whole truth?"

"There are times," I said, "when it would be better if you didn't make any suggestions to people because those people might turn out to be enemies of Uncle Amos. They might try to manipulate things so that anything you said would be twisted and distorted so it would hurt Amos. I think that's the reason you should be very careful not to

114

give out any information at this time. And you must go to the hospital now and make a payment on account of costs."

Sandra looked at her mother in perplexity. Eleanore thought things over for a moment, then said, "Very well, I guess you're right."

"But I don't understand, Mother," Sandra said.

"Just remember what Mr. Lam has told us, Sandra. We won't say anything to anyone. We'll go out now and do some shopping."

"I'll be on my way," I said.

"You're going to your office now?"

"To the office."

"And you haven't told your partner anything about . . . about us?"

"What partner?"

"Mrs. Cool."

"Oh, she's my *business* partner," I said. "I'm just working here as a *friend*. Everything I did for you I did on my own time on a friendly basis. There isn't any charge on the partnership books and no record that the partnership has anything to do with you. Remember that. You've never hired a detective."

I smiled at them, went out and drove to the office.

I walked directly into Bertha Cool's private office.

As it happened, Bertha Cool was holding in her hand the post card I had sent her from Carver City.

She looked up, saw me and her face flushed.

"What the hell's the idea?"

"What idea?"

"Sending me post cards from Carver City."

"I thought you'd like to know where I was."

"Why should I give a damn where you are? I want to know what you're doing."

"All right. I sent you a post card so you'd know what I was doing."

"Why the post card?"

"It's free."

Bertha snorted. "Never mind the wisecracks. What the hell's happened with the Beckley case?"

"We found him."

"With the blonde?"

I shook my head.

"Dead?"

"That's right."

"How did he die?"

"Somebody massaged the back of his head with a jack handle."

"How nice!" Bertha said.

"Isn't it!"

"Who was it?"

"Pay your money and take your choice," I said. "It could have been either the blond hitchhiker or the man he had picked up. Or it could have been both, working together. Or it might have been a fellow by the name of Tom Allcn who was on duty nights at a repair shop at Rommelly. He could have gone out with the repair car, got into an argument with Beckley, cracked him over the head, found that Beckley was loaded, and disposed of the body. It could have been any one of a number of things. We weren't hired to find the murderer, we were hired to find the victim."

"And we found him?"

I nodded.

"Any question about it? I mean, the identity."

"I don't think so. They'll be able to get fingerprints."

"Have you told our client?"

"I told her."

"Get the bonus?"

"Not yet," I said. "We wait until the identification has been conclusively established, but we've done our work. We've found the body."

The phone rang, and Bertha Cool's diamonds made a glittering semicircle as she picked up the receiver and said, "Hello . . . yes, this is Bertha Cool. . . . Donald Lam . . .? The *Tribune?* All right."

She handed me the phone. "The *Tribune* calling."

"Lam?" the reporter's voice asked.

"That's right."

The reporter at the *Tribune* who had talked with me in the Beckley apartment said, "You did me a good turn, Lam. I'm doing you one."

"Fine," I said. "What is it?"

"The police have picked up a suspect in the Beckley murder case."

"A good lead?"

"Hell, he's red hot! They've got the deadwood on him."

"Who is it?" I asked.

"His name is Amos Gage. They picked him up in Mojave, trying to hitchhike a ride to Los Angeles. They gave him a routine questioning, and the answers aroused suspicion. He's been identified."

"Where is he now?"

"Enroute to Bakersfield. It should make quite a story. I thought I'd let you know."

"Thanks," I told him, and hung up.

I turned to Bertha and said, "Well, I guess you can handle it from here, Bertha. It's just a question of billing."

"Where are you going?"

"Bakersfield, and then to Reno."

"Why?" she asked suspiciously.

"So I can return a rented car I left in Bakersfield and pick up the agency car."

"A *rented* car?" Bertha yelled.

"That's right."

"Phone them!" Bertha said. "Why the hell should we take all that time and drive a hundred-odd miles—And why did you want to rent a car in the first place?"

"To save time."

"Where's the agency car?"

"Reno, Nevada."

"What in hell were you doing in Reno?"

"Investigating the Beckley case."

Bertha glared. "How much expense money have you used up?"

"Just about all of it," I said.

Bertha all but collapsed. "I should have known it. You're always going out and getting a check for expense money, grabbing everything in sight and telling me that you'll account for it and turn back the balance. There's never been any balance yet that I can remember."

"Were you to keep the rest of the expenses," I asked, "or turn back any money that wasn't spent to Mrs. Beckley?"

"Don't be silly," Bertha said. "We don't turn back expense money."

"Why not?"

"Well, with you on the job there never is anything to turn back."

"But you wouldn't turn it back anyway," I said. "And really, Mrs. Beckley is entitled to it—if there had been any balance. It's fortunate that there wasn't."

"You're going to Bakersfield and then you're going to Reno?"

"That's right."

"And then driving back from Reno?"

"Uh-huh."

Bertha said, "That doesn't make our bonus look so good."

"I'm entitled to per diem all the time I'm gone until I get back. Don't forget that when you come to make the settlement."

"I won't forget anything," Bertha said, "but don't go raiding the till for any more expense money and don't gamble in Reno—I'll bet you spent a lot of money gambling."

"Not me," I said.

"You mean you didn't spend a dime in those gambling establishments?"

"Oh, sure," I said. "I put money in to see the Prospector's Vision."

"The what?"

"The Prospector's Vision."

"What the hell is a prospector's vision?"

"You drop two bits," I said, "and look through a couple

118

of lenses. You see dawn coming on the desert, then you see a woman with nothing on except a loose red silk handkerchief, and then a breeze comes and blows up the handkerchief and the lights go out."

"And you spent two bits looking at *that?*" Bertha demanded.

"A dollar," I said. "I tried it four times to see if they'd forget to turn out the lights at the proper time."

I eased out of the door, leaving Bertha completely speechless. For once she was too mad and too flabbergasted to throw a fit.

11

I GOT TO BAKERSFIELD AND HAD TO COOL my heels until my friend, Harvey Clover, the undersheriff, returned from Mojave with his prisoner.

The sheriff's office had a plane at its disposal and they transported Amos Gage directly from Bishop to Bakersfield.

Prior to that time, however, they had tried to sweat a story out of him in Mojave.

There were, of course, some reporters and photographers representing the local press, and Frank Malone, my friendly reporter from the Los Angeles *Tribune,* was there to cover the story for his paper.

I watched the plane come in. Gage looked at me and I gave no sign of recognition. He kept his face straight ahead. The sheriff and the undersheriff posed for pictures. They had Gage facing the cameras. They had both of his hands handcuffed so he couldn't throw up an arm to protect himself from the photographers.

They took Gage to the jail and gave interviews to the reporters. I sat in on the interviews.

Harvey Clover did the talking.

"The case started," he said, "when an unidentified body was discovered as the result of a tip from Donald Lam, a private investigator from Los Angeles, who was working on an insurance matter.

"The office took immediate steps to get to the scene of the crime, and it was conclusively established that the man had been murdered. Within a few hours, thanks to the technical skill of our laboratory, we were able to make a positive identification of the body as being that of Malcolm G. Beckley of Los Angeles. From that point on we went into rapid action.

"Beckley had disappeared sometime during the night of the fifth or the early morning hours of the sixth. His car was a Roadracer with license number NFE 801. We broadcast a description of that car and then carried on our investigation along other fronts.

"A key witness, going under the name of Tom Allen, residing at Rommelly, was interrogated, was caught in a mesh of falsehoods and was speedily identified as being a parole violator from Nevada. He was apprehended on parole violation and is being held here on that charge.

"Lie detector tests proved that Tom Allen has some knowledge of facts connected with the murder. He has confessed to a series of actions which may or may not make him at least an accessory to the crime.

"You may state that we are searching for a woman who was in a café at Central Creek up until a short time ago. This woman was going under the name of Edith Jordan, a waitress. She is about twenty-five years of age, about five-feet-three or five-feet-four inches in height and weighs between a hundred and twenty and a hundred and twenty-four pounds. She is probably a natural brunette whose hair has been bleached. She has worked as a waitress and, since she was without funds when she started to work, has drawn small sums in advance. As she left hurriedly without waiting for her pay check, we have reason to believe she will have to apply for work immediately.

"Her connection with the murder is not known, but it is known that Beckley had picked up a woman of approximately that description on the road between Carver City and Central Creek the night he was murdered.

"Once we had put out a general bulletin on the Road-racer, license number NFE 801, we got prompt action. The California Highway Patrol located the car parked just outside of Bridgeport and headed toward Nevada. However, the man who had left the car had not been very clever. He had driven from Nevada into California and actually was headed toward Bishop. Then he swung the car off the road onto the gravel shoulder and made a U-turn. When he did so, the tires picked up dust and fine soil on the shoulder of the road and enough of the dust was carried onto the paved highway by the tires so that it could be determined the car had been put into a U-turn, then driven about a hundred yards down the highway where it was abandoned as though it had been left by a driver who was headed toward Reno but who had run out of gasoline.

"The gasoline tank was bone dry, but there were fresh tool marks on the drain plug in the bottom of the tank and we found where the tank had been drained. The car had than been operated on the small amount of gas that was left in the carburetor.

"All in all we had a fairly complete picture of an individual who had come from the direction of Reno but who had tried to convince us that he had come from the south and had run out of gasoline.

"The car was, of course, immediately processed for fingerprints. It appeared that the driver had been very careful to remove fingerprints but had fallen into one of the most obvious of all errors. Having wiped the steering wheel, the various levers, the handles of the doors, the glass and all parts where he thought he might have left a fingerprint, he had completely forgotten that after he started driving the car, he had adjusted the rearview mirror and in doing so had left fingerprints on the back of the rearview mirror.

"Experts found two fingerprints which are unquestionably those of Amos Gage, the man who is at present under arrest.

"Because we were able to get a very good description of the male hitchhiker Beckley had picked up at the service station in Carver City, we broadcast a description of Amos Gage and concentrated particularly on towns south of Bridgeport, feeling that he had tried to throw the police off the trail by indicating he was headed north when actually he planned to go south.

"A check with the agricultural quarantine station on the California-Nevada boundary showed that the Road-racer car had been driven through there by a man who answered the description of the hitchhiker we were looking for.

"Police were alerted at Bishop, Mojave and Lancaster, told to check carefully on all hitchhikers on the road, on all transients who were unable to give a satisfactory account of themselves.

"Amos Gage was picked up along with fifty or sixty others, fingerprints were taken which proved conclusively that his fingers had left the prints on the back of the rearview mirror of the Beckley automobile. Gage has maintained a steadfast silence, refuses to make any comment whatever until he has been given an opportunity to consult an attorney.

"That covers the situation pretty much to date. Now then, are there any questions?"

One of the reporters said, "Are you going to give him an opportunity to consult an attorney or are you going to keep working on him?"

Clover grinned. "We'll correct your statement about *keep working on him.* Let us say that we plan to give him every opportunity to establish his innocence if he is in fact innocent."

"What about letting him see a lawyer?"

"He is entitled to counsel at all stages of the proceedings," Clover said virtuously, "but in all probablility he will not be legally entitled to use the telephone to call a lawyer until after he has been booked and formally charged with murder."

"When will that be?" Frank Malone asked. And then added, "I'm from the Los Angeles *Tribune*."

"We really can't say," Clover said.

"In other words, you have this guy dead to rights," Malone said. "Is that it?"

"We are arranging to have a service station operator from Carver City arrive here to make a personal identification. We *know* that this man has been driving Beckley's car."

"What about Beckley's belongings?"

"We have been unable to find any property which can be *positively* identified as belonging to Beckley on him, but we have found something over a thousand dollars in currency and it was known that Beckley carried a large amount of money on his person when he was out on selling trips.

"Now, fellows, that just about puts you up to date. We'll keep you posted. Frank Lennox, who operated the service station in Carver City when Beckley picked up a hitchhiker, should be here at any minute. We'll let you know what happens."

Frank Malone slammed his book shut and beat it for a telephone to phone in his story to a rewrite man. The others, being local reporters, were in no great hurry to get to their papers. They wanted to wait until deadline and see if the story developed.

"Find out anything about where this fellow had been keeping himself during the past week or so?" I asked Clover when the newspaper reporters had left.

"Not a thing—Look, Lam, you've worked on this case. You know the facts pretty well. How would you like to take a crack at him?"

"I doubt if I could do a damned bit of good," I said. "At least at the present time. You folks go ahead and work on him and then if it's hopeless I may be able to get something."

I left the room, walked down to a phone booth where Frank Malone was telephoning in his story and waited.

When he was all ready to hang up I knocked on the door.

Malone opened the telephone booth. "Something new, Donald?" he asked.

"You've got it right there in your morgue," I said.

"Got what?"

"A whale of a story on this guy, Amos Gage. Marlene Hyde knows all about it."

"What about it?"

"Gage is a beneficiary under a spendthrift trust running somewhere around half to three-quarters of a million dollars. He gets all of the money turned over to him absolutely within a period of about two weeks unless he has in the meantime been convicted of some major crime, in which event the money all goes to various charitable organizations who would doubtless be glad to buy papers to read about it."

Malone's eyes got wide. "Are you kidding?"

"Ask for the morgue," I said. "Get Marlene Hyde on the line."

Malone turned back to the telephone so excited that he could hardly talk. "Hold it," he yelled. "This may be one hell of a story—human interest, drama, suspense, God knows what! Put me through to the library right away. I want Marlene Hyde, and wait on the line and listen."

A few seconds later he said, "Hello! Marlene? This is Frank Malone. I'm over at Bakersfield. I'm talking with a private investigator by the name of Donald Lam—says you know him. . . . Uh-huh. . . . Oh, he did, eh . . . ? Amos Gage is the name we're looking for and—You got them there . . . ? All right, turn them over to rewrite, the whole damned story. . . . Holy humped-up suffering mackerel! What a yarn . . . ! Hell, yes. . . . You on the line, Jim . . . ? You got all this stuff from Marlene . . . ? God, yes! What a whale of a story! Put some sob sisters on it and let's go to work. Interview the persons who will be the beneficiaries in the event Gage loses his inheritance. Get hold of the trustee. Find out where Gage was living and see who his friends are, what he's been doing. . . . My God, this is a natural! Sure, they've got a dead open-and-shut case against the guy. The only thing is, can they get the wheels turning so they can get a conviction here within the two-week period? If they can't do it, Gage will be thirty-five and comes into all the money —and we're the only ones that are in on the story. My God, it's an exclusive . . . ! Hell, yes! I'll be camping right here on the job. The next development will be an identification by Frank Lennox, who works in Carlyle Kamp's Service Station in Carver City. He's due here any minute."

Malone listened for a while, then said, "That's right. Now, look, get this straight. The sheriff's office here has done some shrewd work but most of it has been the result of tips by Donald Lam of the firm of Cool & Lam, and he's been playing ball with us. It's through him we've got an exclusive on this. . . . Now, look, I'm going to call the wire services and peddle the story as soon as we get on the street. We want the first edition. . . . Atta boy . . . ! Okay, I'll wait thirty minutes."

Malone came out of the telephone booth and started pumping my hand up and down. "What a whale of a story, Donald!" he said. "And we're sitting right on top of it —the city editor didn't much like the idea of my coming over here. I told him I thought it could be developed into a hell of a big story with a local angle, but I had to press a little bit to get here. Now we're sitting on top of the heap with an exclusive that is going to make our rivals look sick."

"That's fine," I said.

"Believe me, Donald, we're going to see you get a spread out of it. They're sending over a photographer and a couple of leg men and a couple of feature writers to do sidebars. Boy, we're sitting on top of the biggest story of the year and we're going to play it to the hilt."

"When'll they be here?"

"Just as quick as they can get here by plane," he said.

"Okay," I told him, "only remember one thing."

"What?"

"I didn't tell you anything about who Gage was. You found that out in your morgue."

"My God, don't you want any of the credit?"

"I don't want credit," I said. "I want publicity, but I don't want Harvey Clover to get sore at me, thinking I held out on him, and I don't want the local press to think that I gave you the story."

Malone hit me on the back so hard that I saw double for two or three seconds.

"Lam," he said, "you're a peach, and by God, you sure know your way around. Publicity! I'll tell the world you'll get publicity!"

"All right," I said. "I get publicity, and the *Tribune* gets the story because of its wide-awake reporters and a city editor who was smart enough to start checking the morgue just as soon as the name of Amos Gage came over the wire."

Frank Malone thought that over for a moment, then dove back into the telephone booth and frantically dialed long distance.

I went down to a restaurant and had a cup of coffee.

A few minutes later Frank Lennox showed up, having been escorted in by motorcycle officers all the way from Carver City.

He was hustled into jail while the sheriff's office arranged for a line-up. Then Clover called the press into another consultation.

"All right, boys," he said. "We've got the thing sewed up now. Frank Lennox says there can be no doubt about it, that this is the man who wanted to hitchhike a ride on the night of the fifth. Because he was a fellow lodge member, Lennox let him sit around the service station."

"What lodge?" one of the reporters asked.

Clover grinned and said, "If I'd wanted you to know that, I'd have told you."

"We'll find out when we interview Lennox," the reporter said.

126

"Sure you will," Clover said. "Then you will have found out from him and not from me, and you're not going to be interviewing Lennox for a while."

"Why not?"

"Because for various reasons we're keeping him sewed up until after we get photographs developed and a written statement from him. However, we can tell you this, that there was a line-up of seven people, and Lenox unhesitatingly picked Amos Gage as the hitchhiker.

"Moreover, Lennox was cautious enough to take down the license number of the automobile that picked Gage up. That license number was the license number on Beckley's car."

"What about Gage? Has he cracked yet?"

"Not yet. He still wants to see his lawyer."

"Is he going to get one?"

"He's going to get a chance to telephone one. We've told him we'll take a message to any attorney he designates. The trouble is he doesn't know any local attorney and he wants to get wised up before he gets somebody."

"Put him in the tank and he'll get wised up fast."

"What do you mean by that crack?" Clover asked.

"It's an educational experience," the reporter said.

"What is?"

"Getting in the tank. . . . What about all this money?"

"It's being held as evidence."

"Can you prove it's Beckley's money?"

"We can't prove it but we can come damned close to it," Clover said. "I tell you, we've got this guy nailed to the mast."

A light came on, on a telephone exchange. Clover picked up the receiver, said, "Yeah," listened for a minute, then said, "Okay."

He hung up the telephone, turned to the representatives of the press and said, "Okay, boys. The guy has asked for a specific attorney. He's asked us to call Goodwin F. James and ask him to come down to the jail right away."

The reporters pushed back their chairs, scurried for the

door, wanting to talk with James before he went into the jail and then again after he came out.

Clover turned to me. "Sure you wouldn't like to take a crack at this fellow, Donald?"

I said, "I'll talk with him but I wouldn't want to go in there as one of your representatives, and, on the other hand, I wouldn't want to hold out anything. Better let it go the way it is."

"You could talk with him privately," Clover said.

"Sure," I said, grinning, "and the room would be bugged."

"Anything wrong with that?"

"Not from *my* standpoint."

"I thought you were co-operating with us."

"I've given you information."

"Well, I've given *you* plenty."

"Then it's a stand-off."

"And remember, any time you want anything around here about all you have to do is ask for it. You're a good egg."

"Thanks," I told him, went down and caught a cab to the airport.

12

BY AUTOMOBILE IT'S A BOTTLENECK NIGHT-mare to go from Sacramento to Reno—up over the summit of the Sierras, down the pass and around the lake where the famous Donner party spent its tragic winter, but it only takes a little over thirty minutes by air.

I puddle-jumped to Sacramento from Bakersfield, then took one of the United Convairs from Sacramento to Reno, picked up the agency car, had something to eat and called Harvey Clover in Bakersfield.

"Lam talking," I said. "What's new with Amos Gage?"

"He has a lawyer."

"Goodwin James?"

"That's right."

"And what does Goodwin James say?"

"Nothing."

"What does his client say?"

"Nothing."

"And what about Tom Allen?"

"Now, there," Clover said, "you have something that puzzles me. I can understand Gage not saying anything. If he opens his mouth he's hooked. Between now and the time of trial, some little discrepancy may appear that will give him a chance to squirm out of it. He'll have his attorney go over all the evidence with a fine-toothed comb. He'll probably wind up by swearing that the blond hitchhiker tried to kill them both and take the car."

"How do you know she didn't?" I asked.

"We don't—not yet," Clover said, "but we do know that someone cashed one of Beckley's traveler's checks at a Reno casino and that it was a man who cashed the check."

"All right," I said. "We were talking about Tom Allen."

"But Tom Allen," he said, "has no reason to clam up. He's not mixed up in a murder—at least he shouldn't be. We don't think he is and we're not going to try to tie him into the murder."

"Are you sure?" I asked.

"Well, we're not making any promises," Clover said, "but Tom has clammed up. We already know the bad thing against him. We've got him dead to rights. He's a parole violator from Nevada, and they'll throw the book at him, but he just sits there and won't talk."

"Won't talk about anything?" I asked.

"He won't talk, period. He doesn't ask for any attorney or anything, he just says, 'No comment.' "

"And the blond waitress?"

"We're going to get her," Clover said. "She can't get away. We've got an all-points bulletin out all over four western states. We're having police check on every restaurant where waitresses are hired on a catch-as-catch-can basis. We're checking with the unions."

"Maybe she's decided to change jobs," I said. "Maybe she's a chambermaid in a hotel now."

"Don't think we haven't thought of that. We're covering every lead. We're going to get her. It may take time but we'll have her."

"How did she get away? Have you found that out?"

"We haven't found out a thing. She walked out of the restaurant and told Pops, the cook, that it was a slack time and he could hold down the place until she got back."

"And then?"

"That's all. She vanished."

"A girl like that could pick up a ride pretty easy."

"Sure, she could pick up a ride. But she's got to light someplace."

"What about her name, social security number, any of that stuff?"

Clover said, "Hell, we aren't wasting any time on her name. She's some tramp who works under a dozen different names. When we work with any of the union registrations, of course, we ask them about Edith Jordan, but that's just on the off-chance she's used the same alias. We are, however, doing a lot of checking on persons whose first name is Edith—You take a waitress like that and they usually keep the same first name. They'll use any one of a dozen different last names, but the first name is usually the same."

"That's right," I agreed.

"Incidentally," Cover said, "we crossed your back trail up there in Reno."

"How come?"

"Weren't you the one who was trying to trace that Beckley traveler's check?"

"That's right."

"You had us worried for a while," Clover said, "then we checked on the description and figured you had to be the one."

"Sure," I said. "I've been trying to pick up Beckley's trail. I told you that."

"But you didn't tell us the murderer had cashed the check."

I said, "At that time I figured it was Beckley who cashed the check."

"Okay, Donald, keep your nose clean," Clover said. "There's nothing much new at this end. The *Tribune* did some good work and broke a big story about Amos Gage. It seems he's going to come into a whole bunch of money under some kind of a trust arrangement if he can keep from being convicted of a crime before he's thirty-five."

"When will he be thirty-five?"

"Inside of two weeks."

"How much chance does he stand of holding out for two weeks?"

Clover laughed and said, "Do you think we're going to play into the guy's hands like that? A dozen different charities stand to benefit thirty thousand bucks apiece if Gage gets convicted before his thirty-fifth birthday. What would you do if you were a district attorney and had a situation like that confronting you?"

I said, "I'd probably try to get him convicted and ask some of these folks how about a campaign contribution."

"You might get elected," Clover said. "Anyway, even if this guy beats the gas chamber, he wouldn't have any use for all that money in prison."

"You can't tell," I said. "He might bribe a guard."

"He could if he could get it in, but the wardens weren't born yesterday. As long as that guy stays in prison, his money will stay outside."

"Okay," I told him. "I'll be seeing you."

I hung up the phone, went out and sat in the agency heap and did some thinking.

That blond waitress hadn't had too much of a head start on the police. They'd been hot on her trail all the way and they hadn't uncovered a damned thing.

When that happens it usually means someone is working on a false premise. Since we'd come down from Rom-

131

melly, everyone thought that the girl must have headed on downgrade and gone through Carver City.

Why wouldn't it have been the smart thing to have headed right back toward Bakersfield?

I was willing to bet that, of the all-points bulletins out, the Bakersfield police weren't doing any checking right within the city of Bakersfield. . . . Still, that would be dangerous. The Bakersfield papers were full of the story.

I started thinking of what I'd do if I had been in the waitress' shoes. The more I thought of it, the more I thought that catching a ride right through to Bakersfield would be the smart thing to do. Then what?

I had several things to go on. She'd known Tom Allen. She'd known him well. Tom Allen was willing to take quite a bit of a rap and quite a bit of police abuse in order to protect her.

Why?

The answer was that he must be protecting himself or else that for some reason she was something very special.

Suppose she was something very special.

I played mental tag with that angle.

Tom Allen had been confined in the state penitentiary at Carson City. If this waitress had been someone rather special, she'd have been near him.

Just on the off-chance, I hunted up the United Airlines.

"I want to get in touch with your stewardesses who made the run from Los Angeles to Sacramento to Reno," I said. "I'm particularly anxious to find out if a certain young woman boarded the plane and came into Reno."

The manager smiled and shook his head. "That would be pretty difficult," he said. "It might be arranged—we can show you the passenger lists, if that will help."

He opened a drawer and pushed through some passenger lists, turning them around so they were right side up to me.

I shook my head and said, "That won't help any. This party might have been—" And then I stopped in midsentence. The name Edith Jordan was staring me right

132

in the face. She'd taken a morning plane from Los Angeles and come right on through to Sacramento and Reno.

"Well, I'm sorry," he said. "It would be quite a job interviewing the stewardesses, but we could arrange it if necessary."

"Well," I told him, "it may not be necessary."

I went to the taxicab company. I located the drivers who had covered the flight in question. I checked around and finally found a cab driver who had picked up the blonde —a girl who had her purse with her and no other baggage. She'd been in a hurry and had taken a cab while other passengers were waiting for the baggage to be unloaded.

I gave him five bucks and he gave me an address.

I went out to the address. It was a pretty fair apartment house. I looked at the name list for any woman whose first name was Edith.

The name was on the mailbox big as life: Edith Jordan.

And then, just to check, I walked over to the telephone booth and looked in the phone book. There she was, Edith Jordan, with a telephone listed in her name.

I started to call her, thought better of it, went up to the apartment and pressed my thumb against the imitation mother-of-pearl call bell.

Chimes sounded on the inside. I waited a minute and pressed the button again.

The door opened a couple of inches, held in place by a gilt chain.

Edith Jordan was looking out at me, and her eyes were big and startled.

"Hello, Miss Jordan," I said. "I had to talk with you, and—"

"I have nothing to say to you," she said, and tried to slam the door.

The chain kept me from getting it open, my foot kept her from getting it closed.

"Get your foot out of the door," she said, "or I'll—"

"Or you'll what?" I asked.

"Get my electric iron and start massaging your toes,"

she said. And then added, almost as an afterthought, "with the sharp point."

"Don't do it," I said. "I wanted to give you a little information." And then added, "Before the police get here."

"The police!" she said.

"Sure. Who did you expect?"

"I have nothing to say to the police."

"That may well be, but they've got a lot to say to you."

"And what did you want to tell me?"

"Something for your own good."

"Just who are you, anyway?"

I fished my credentials out of my pocket and held them so she could see them through the crack in the door. "Donald Lam," I said.

"A detective?"

"Private."

"What are you working on?"

"Getting in to see you at the moment."

"Well, you certainly work hard enough," she said. "Take your foot out of the door so I can close it, and I'll pull the chain out of the catch and let you in."

"You wouldn't change your mind once you got the door closed?" I asked.

"Listen," she said, "when I promise I'm going to do anything, I do it. If I'm going anywhere, I go all the way. I either don't start or I finish."

"Good girl," I said, and took my foot out of the door.

She closed the door. I heard the rattle of the chain, then she opened the door and said, "Come on in."

It was a nice apartment. She evidently rented it furnished, but there were lots of little personal touches which indicated she'd been there for some time.

I looked the place over and did some mental arithmetic. In Reno, where women come to take up a six-week residence, there are quite a few furnished apartments. There are also a lot of motels rented by the week. They get money for them.

"In Reno," I said, "this thing costs money."

134

"Are *you* telling *me?*" she asked. "Sit down. Can I buy you a drink?"

I shook my head.

"All right, give. What should I know before the police get here?"

I said, "I shouldn't tell you this, and I don't want you to tell anyone."

"All right, I'll play fair with you, you play fair with me. What have to got to tell me?"

"Tom Allen," I said.

"What about him?"

"He isn't saying a word. The police are bringing all sorts of pressure to bear on him and he won't say a word. They're moving heaven and earth trying to find you, and Tom is sitting tight."

"If he sits tight," she said, "the police won't know anything about me."

"How do you suppose I found you?" I asked.

"Tom didn't tell you?"

"I haven't' seen him since the police put him on a lie detector and showed that he was lying when he said he didn't know you."

"Oh-oh," she said in dismay. "Then the police *will* be here."

"Probably."

"That," she said, "could be bad."

"Why? On account of the murder?"

"What murder?"

"You don't know?"

She shook her head.

I had clippings from one of the early editions of the Bakersfield paper. I took them from my pocket and let her read through them.

She settled back in her chair, crossed her knees without going through the formality of pulling down her skirt for the sixteenth of an inch that shows an attempt at modesty. She had good legs and she knew it, and she'd let me into the apartment. I was a friend. She read the clippings and I looked at a wonderful pair of legs.

She leaned forward and handed me the clippings. I took them.

She said, "That complicates the situation, doesn't it?"

"It does."

"I don't know anything about it."

"Flight," I said, "is an evidence of guilt."

"I wasn't running away from any murder rap. I . . . I suppose I could be an accessory on parole violation, and I guess they could make some kind of a morals charge against me—I'm being fair with you, Donald, and putting cards on the table."

"I like what I've seen so far," I said. "Put out some more."

She said, "Tom isn't a bad sort. He's impulsive and emotional and—well, as far as women are concerned, he's what you'd call a pushover. I don't suppose he can help it, he's a man. Women are different from men. They go for one man and that's the man in their lives.

"Tom wasn't a one-woman man. He'd try to be, and I think he tried in good faith, but when some babe would throw herself at him, he'd go overboard."

"And that was what your fight was about?" I asked.

"That was what my fight was about."

"Tell me."

She said, "Tom and I were engaged. We were going to be married. But he was a restless individual. I'd been married before, and the first thing I knew I was traveling with him. We were going as man and wife. Then he got drunk and got into trouble. Reno was his undoing. He started gambling and won about three hundred dollars one night. Boy, we sure lived it up. He was wanting to know why no one had told him about this easy way of making a living."

"So the next night he went back to the tables and lost everything," I said.

She nodded. "He lost his shirt and cashed a check. That's where he made his mistake. People up here frown on giving bad checks to gamblers, and the gamblers control the state."

"So Tom went to prison. And what did you do?"

"Stuck around and waited," she said.

"How did you support yourself?"

She started to say something, changed her mind, looked me in the eyes and said, "Tom doesn't know this. I have money."

"How much?"

"A reasonable amount. I don't want Tom to know. Tom's temperament is such that it would ruin him if he could latch onto a woman who furnished him with all the necessities of life.

"Tom doesn't like to have me work as a waitress. I'm friendly and my proportions aren't exactly displeasing to the average male. When you're waiting tables some of the people are just friendly, some of them are fresh and some of them . . . some of them pinch."

"Go on," I said.

"So," she said, "I'd leave it up to Tom to support me. Tom is a pretty good garage mechanic. He can make a living all right when he wants to, and he's got the makings of a mighty fine man when he settles down. But he's wild. He's restless and . . . well, anyway, that's it. He went to prison at Carson City and I waited. He got out on parole.

"Now, that's one thing that you have to keep in mind. The conditions of parole are that you can't leave a state, and Nevada has legalized gambling, and legalized gambling and Tom don't mix. I knew it and he knew it.

"Of course, one of the conditions of the parole was that he was to stay away from places where liquor was sold and stay away from gambling and those things, but Tom couldn't do it. The first thing I knew he'd gone to the crap tables and he won about eighty-five dollars.

"He came home and told me about it. I knew what that meant, and after he got to thinking it over, he knew what it meant. I told him there was only one thing to do and that was to go to California and get a job."

"You're calling him Tom," I said.

"Tom's his first name. Allen isn't his last name."

137

"What is it?"

"Adair."

"But you kept the apartment here?"

"I kept the apartment here and he doesn't know it."

"Why?"

"My things are here. Tom never did know about this apartment. He thought I was working in a restaurant waiting tables while he was in prison. He didn't need to know about this, and I didn't tell him."

"You have ample money to keep it up?"

"I have ample money to keep it up," she said.

"All right," I told her. "Now let's find out about the night of the fifth and the morning of the sixth."

"There wasn't anything to it," she said. "Tom and I were living in a motel in Rommelly. He worked nights at the garage. It was the only job he could get. I'd come around about seven-thirty in the morning when he got off and we'd go out and have breakfast. Then we'd go to the motel and he'd sleep. I'd try to keep things quiet for him for two or three hours. That was all the sleep he needed. Sometimes he didn't need that much.

"You see, he was on duty nights. He had to sit up until midnight, but he closed the doors at nine o'clock and would listen to the radio. Then he could go to bed at midnight. Sometimes he'd get calls during the night—mostly it was to sell gasoline. He'd go out to the pumps and fill up tanks for motorists who were accustomed to driving in more populated countries and let their gas tanks get empty, or motorists who thought they'd find an all-night service station and found the town closed up with the sidewalks all rolled up."

"Go on," I told her.

"There isn't a lot more to tell," she said. "On the morning of the sixth, about quarter past seven, I walked into the garage to pick Tom up. . . . He wasn't expecting me."

"You mean another woman was there?"

"Another woman *had* been there."

"How did you know?"

"Lots of ways."

"Can you tell me some?"

She thought for a moment, then said, "Some."

"All right," I said, "what were the some?"

"He hadn't washed up the coffee cups," she said. "One of them had lipstick around it.

"There's a washbasin there and hot water. Tom usually shaved about quarter past seven, just before he was due to go off work so he'd be clean-shaven to go to breakfast with me. This time there was lipstick on his shaving mirror."

"What do you mean?" I asked.

"She'd been making up in front of his little shaving mirror," she said, "and she'd got lipstick on it."

"How would a girl get lipstick on a shaving mirror?"

"You know how a woman makes up her mouth. She puts the lipstick on and then she molds it into position with her little finger."

"Go ahead," I said.

"Well, of course, her little finger had lipstick all over it, and she picked up Tom's mirror to look at herself and make sure she was presentable when she left, and left smudges of lipstick on the back of the mirror where her little finger touched it."

"That's interesting," I said. "What became of the mirror?"

"I took it."

I thought that over. "Where is it now?"

She got up, crossed the room, opened the drawer, took out a purse, and handed me a reversible round shaving mirror of the kind that can be purchased in drugstores and twenty-five-cent stores. It was rather a cheap affair with a wire handle; one side was a plain mirror, one side was slightly concave so it gave a magnified image.

"She had used the side that gave the magnified image," Edith said. "This is the plain side of the mirror. You can see the red imprints of her little finger."

I studied the reverse side of the mirror. Not only were there imprints of the little finger in lipstick, but in one place

139

there was a perfect print of the ridges and whorls. One other print wasn't quite so plain but could still be identified.

I said, "Do you have any transparent Scotch tape here?"

"I think so."

"Get it."

She got it. "What are you going to do?"

"I'll show you," I said.

I cut off several pieces of the transparent Scotch tape and pasted them over the fingerprints on the mirror.

"What's the idea?" she asked.

"Put your initials on here," I said, "and the date."

She did it.

"That will preserve those prints from being smudged," I said. "It's a wonder you haven't rubbed them off in your purse. Why did you save this mirror?"

"Tom doesn't know I have it," she said. "I accused him of having a woman there, and at first he lied to me and then he said she hadn't come in but had waited in the doorway while he was getting dressed, that he had made a cup of coffee, she asked him for one and he took it to the door and handed it to her, that she drank the coffee and handed him the empty cup and he took it back and put it on the table."

"So what?"

"So," she said, "while he was telling me that fairy story, I took his mirror as proof and slipped it in my purse."

"And then what?"

"Then," she said, "I walked out on him. I told him when he got ready to tell the truth, he could try and look for me. I told him I was finished—and at the time I thought I was."

"And what did you do?"

"Hitchhiked to Central Creek, went in there for breakfast. Dorothy Lennox was waiting on tables and running herself ragged. She'd had to come in the night before. There were a lot of fishermen on the road, the place had been busy, and Pops wouldn't do the cooking and the table-hopping both. He couldn't."

"So what?"

"So I got a job. I felt it wouldn't be too long before Tom would hear about me table-hopping down there and then he'd be down. It wasn't too far away for him to come down without losing his job—and, well, if he'd been properly repentant, I'd have forgiven him and gone back. It's the way those things always happen. He philanders and sometimes I catch him at it and sometimes I don't. Usually I know when he's been philandering—a woman can tell."

"Does he always lie about it?"

"Always."

"Then you have a fight and leave him?"

"I haven't left him before. We've had fights and I've threatened to leave him. Then we've had reconciliations. He's promised not to do it again. Women are his weakness. I know it. He knows it. Tom is wild, he's emotional. He hasn't settled down yet but he's a good egg underneath and . . . well, Mr. Lam, it happens the guy is in my hair and I can't get him out."

I got up and said, "Here's my card. The safest place for you is right here. Forget that you've seen me and I'll forget that I've seen you. Now, no matter what happens, *stay right here.* Don't let anything stampede you. No matter what you hear, just stay here."

"Wouldn't it be better if I—"

"It would be a hell of a lot worse," I told her. "Flight is evidence of guilt, and you can't tell what they're going to charge you with. As long as you're here, you haven't resorted to flight. You simply got mad at your boy friend and walked out of the restaurant where you were working. . . . What did you do, hitchhike to—?"

"I followed you folks right up the grade," she said. "I walked out within five minutes after you left. I told Pops to keep an eye on the place. I just walked out and thumbed a ride and we were right behind you when you drove into Rommelly."

"You didn't stop there?"

"My ride took me right on through to Bakersfield. Then he gassed up there and we went to Los Angeles."

"You were with him all the way?"

"I was with him all the way," she said. "It was something of an ordeal. I got pawed and I had to string him along. I told him I had a boy friend in Los Angeles who was expecting me but I liked him better and that if he'd let me go and hand my boy friend a line, I'd come back and meet him—I guess the guy's waiting yet."

"Then what?"

"I took a taxi to the airport, got on one of the United planes and came here."

"Proving," I said, "that sheer simplicity and direct action is a damned sight better than all the chicanery in the world."

"You think that proves it?" she asked.

"I think that proves it."

"You know, Donald," she said, *"you're* a pretty good egg."

"You're a good egg yourself," I said. "First thing tomorrow morning you go to a lawyer. Tell him that you have a piece of evidence you want to preserve. Let him think it's in a divorce case. Tell him you aren't ready to consult him yet, but you want him to help preserve the evidence. Show him the mirror with the fingerprint outlines in lipstick. Get him to put his initials and the date next to yours on the Scotch tape you've put over the mirror. Get him to seal it in an envelope and lock it in his safe."

"Then what?" she asked.

"Then," I said, "return here and resume the even tenor of your existence. You're sure Tom doesn't know anything about this apartment?"

She shook her head. "He's never been here. I never let him know anything about it."

"You've had it all the time he was in prison?"

"Just about."

"You let him think you were working in a restaurant?"

She nodded.

"And after he got out, what happened?"

"I let him get a job and get a place for us to live."

"Much of a place?"

"It was a stinking place," she said. "It was a dirty little shack—but it was home."

"You used to sneak away and come up here sometimes to get really cleaned up and—"

"I never sneaked away, Donald. That shack was home, he was my man, I stayed with him and stayed with the house and did the best I could with it."

"Good girl," I told her. "Remember the advice I gave you."

She came to the door with me, gave me her hand and then, on a sudden impulse, tilted up her cheek for me to kiss. "You're a sweet kid, Donald," she said.

"You're all right yourself," I told her.

I went back to the agency heap and started the long drive for Bakersfield.

13

GOODWIN F. JAMES WAS A TALL, RAWBONED, gangling individual with high cheekbones, a big bony nose, and clothes that hung loosely from his frame. The face was dominated by the eyes, deep-set gray eyes that peered out from under black bushy eyebrows and seemed to throw jets of ice water.

"I'm glad to meet you, Lam," he said. "My client keeps talking about you."

"Indeed?" I asked.

"That's right. I'm wondering why he places so much importance on your opinion and advice."

"I haven't given him my opinion and I didn't know he wanted my advice."

"He does."

"How? When? Where? Why?"

"He wants it as soon as he can get it, but I don't know just how to arrange it where there could be a completely confidential discussion—you'll understand anything my client might say to you wouldn't be a privileged communication. I wouldn't want him to say some of the things to you, for instance, that he has said to me."

"Why not?"

"It would be bad for his case."

"You mean he's made certain admissions?"

James didn't answer my question but said instead, "Can you tell me why it is my client places such a high value on your advice?"

I shook my head.

"You're not an attorney?"

"I've had legal training."

"The devil!"

I nodded.

"You haven't presumed to advise him, have you?"

I looked at him with wide-eyed candor and said, "When would I have met your client?"

"That," he said, "is one of the things I want to put together. Now then, I have been instructed by my client to get in touch with you and ask you certain questions."

"Such as what?"

"Such as whether you think a jury will believe his story."

"That's for you to decide," I said.

"That's what I told Gage, but he has insisted that I discuss it with you."

"Well, what do you think?" I asked.

"It's not my province to express views on the outcome of criminal cases in which my clients are involved."

"Quite true," I said cheerfully, "and by the same sign, it's not my province to express my views on the outcome of cases in which your clients are involved."

"Oh, hell, Lam!" he said. "Let's quit beating around the bush. When did you see Gage?"

"If I had seen Gage," I said, "while the police were searching for him and hadn't reported the fact, I'd be in an embarrassing position, wouldn't I?"

"I would say so."

"I don't like to be in an embarrassing position."

James put big-knuckled, bony hands on the blotter of his desk, spreading his fingers apart, pressing down with the palms on the blotter, rubbing the palms of his hands gently back and forth. "You're a hard man to interview," he said.

"You're getting a lot more than you're giving," I told him.

Abruptly he looked up and said, "In what I am about to tell you I am following the instructions of my client. I am doing so against my better judgment."

I didn't say anything.

"My client wants to plead guilty," he said.

"Guilty!" I exclaimed.

He nodded lugubriously.

"To what?"

"To first-degree murder."

"What the hell!" I said.

"If he should plead guilty," James said, "the chances are about even money that he'd get life imprisonment. However, by the same token the chances are about fifty-fifty that the judge would sentence him to death."

"No deal with the district attorney?" I asked.

"He wants me to make a deal with the district attorney."

"On life imprisonment?"

"I would try to make such a deal if it could be arranged, but that isn't what he is primarily interested in."

"What is it?"

"He wants to have the case continued until after the first of the month. At that time he will be thirty-five years of age and if he has not been convicted of any major crime by that time he is absolutely entitled to a fortune."

"What good is a fortune going to do a corpse?" I asked.

"I've asked him that question," James said. "He tells me that he wants a Mrs. Eden to have the money, that if he goes to prison he'll give her a large chunk of the money, that if he dies he'll leave it all to her by his will—and,

145

of course, he has offered me a very handsome fee if I will arrange the matter and will see that the money due him is paid over from the trust fund."

"And if he doesn't plead guilty?" I asked. "And no deal is made?"

"Then we have a very peculiar situation. The district attorney is rushing this case to trial and I may state that he seems to have the full co-operation of the Court. There is an unseemly haste in getting this matter placed on the calendar—of course you can realize why."

I nodded.

"Well," James said, "what do you think?"

I said, "If he goes to trial and is convicted, do you think he will be convicted before his thirty-fifth birthday?"

"I feel certain that the trial will be so expedited that he will have been convicted of a major crime before his thirty-fifth birthday."

"In that event he gets nothing."

James nodded.

"And in that event, you get nothing."

Again he nodded.

"But if he pleads guilty and an arrangement is made with the district attorney that the case will be continued until after his thirty-fifth birthday and before the plea is taken, you will then get a sizable fee, I take it."

He nodded.

"Say fifty thousand?" I asked.

"Oh, no, no! Not that much!" he said. "Heavens, no! I wouldn't think of charging the man *that* much, particularly when all I did for him was to offer a plea of guilty on his behalf. I would consider that an exorbitant fee."

"But you've got to supervise the collection of the money from the trust fund."

"There shouldn't be any difficulty with that."

"You don't know the trustee."

"Well, I'd take a chance on that."

"You mind telling me what your fee is?"

He clenched the big hands into fists, then spread the

146

fingers again and looked down at the blotter. "Thirty-five," he said.

"Thirty-five what?"

"Thirty-five thousand."

I waited a minute for the facts to soak in and said, "So your client wants to plead guilty and either go to prison or go to the gas chamber. If you advise him you can make a deal and he's to plead guilty, you're thirty-five thousand bucks winner, and you haven't had very much work.

"If he goes to trial, you have to do a lot of work and you probably won't get a red cent."

"I hadn't analyzed my own position in the matter quite that clearly."

"The hell you hadn't!" I said.

"All right, then," he admitted. "I'd thought about it. What's wrong with that?"

"Nothing. The question is, what's for your client's best interests?"

"He wants to do some good in the world," James said. "He tells me that as he looks back on his life he's done nothing to help himself or to help the world. He's wasted his opportunities and has become a typical periodic alcoholic. He feels that prison might do him some good and he feels that he can definitely be of service if he has money with which to do good."

"What will the district attorney do? Will he let him wait until after he's thirty-five in order to plead?"

"I don't know. I have an idea the district attorney might consider a proposition along those lines."

"But you haven't made it?"

"No."

I sat and watched him, and James balled his fingers up into fists again and the skin grew white across his knuckles.

At length he looked up at me and said, "What do you think of his chances?"

"Of his chances of what?"

"You know what I mean—before a jury."

I said, "If he tells his story and there's no corroboration, he isn't going to get acquitted."

James nodded.

"On the other hand," I said, "there are twelve jurors. I would say he stood one chance in twelve of getting it believed, perhaps two chances in twelve."

"You mean a hung jury?"

"That's the way I'd estimate it."

"Well," James said, "that wouldn't do him any good. He'd have the whole blamed thing to go over with again after he—"

"After he became rich," I said.

"Yes," James said, "that's true."

I said, "Then he could pay you a good fee for your services, he could get experts and he could—"

"Hire detectives," James said eagerly.

"That isn't what *I* said," I told him.

"It's what *I* said," he announced.

"Well," I told him, "Gage wanted you to talk it over with me. You've talked it over with me."

"You wouldn't plead guilty?"

"Hell, no!"

"You realize the chances, Mr. Lam?"

"Sure, I realize the chances. I'd take them."

"I'm glad I've had this opportunity to talk with you," he said. "I shall convey your ideas to my client."

"Just what kind of a case have they got against him?" I asked. And then added, "So far."

"Quite a case," James admitted.

"Want to outline it?"

James picked up a lead pencil which was lying on the desk, wrapped his big fingers around it, pulled over a pad of paper and on it, with the pencil, wrote the figure one and put a circle around it.

"First," he said, "they have an absolute identification of Amos Gage as being the man who went to Carlyle Kamp's Service Station at Carver City and got a ride with Malcolm G. Beckley—and there can't be any doubt about it, because the operator at the service station made a note of Beckley's license number."

I nodded.

James put down the figure two and drew a circle around that.

"Next, Beckley stopped at Central Creek and telephoned his wife again. He called her first from Carver City. He called her the second time from Central Creek. The first time he told her that he was going to have to go on to Reno. The second time, when he called her from Central Creek, he told her that he not only had the hitchhiker he'd picked up a Carver City, but that he had a blonde with him, another hitchhiker he'd picked up, that he was making her ride in the back seat."

"Can the district attorney introduce evidence of those phone conversations?" I said. "Aren't they hearsay?"

"There, of course, is a problem," James admitted. "We'll fight like hell on it, but the defendant was sitting there at the counter at the time the phone call from Central Creek was put in."

"Who says he was?" I asked.

James looked at me and took his long bony fingers and rubbed the finger tips along the angle of his jaw. "Now *there,*" he said, "you've got a point. They can't find that waitress. Of course, you know and I know the defendant was there, but the question is, can they prove it? That's the point."

James took the pencil and marked a big question mark after number two.

He wrote down the number three and drew a big circle around it. "At Carver City the defendant was broke. He didn't have a dime. He didn't have the price of a cup of coffee. He told the service station attendant so. When he was picked up by the police he had nearly twelve hundred dollars on him. Evidence will show that Beckley carried large sums of money in his possession and it's pretty good evidence that the defendant got the money from Beckley."

"Suppose he got it from gambling?"

"What did he gamble with?"

I said, "He could have found ten bucks."

"He *could* have," James said, without enthusiasm.

James picked up the pencil again and the phone rang.

He said, "Excuse me," picked up the receiver and said, "Hello. This is Goodwin F. James talking . . . yes, go right ahead."

He glanced at me.

The receiver made noises and continued to make noises. James sat there listening. His face twisted with expression for a moment, then became a mask, but his right hand gripped the pencil until the wood snapped in two. He threw the pieces of the pencil angrily into a wastebasket, said into the telephone, "You're absolutely certain," waited a while, then said, "Well, I guess that does it."

He said good-by and dropped the receiver into place.

"All right," I said, "I take it you have a couple more numbers to put down on that pad."

By way of answer he picked up the pad, ripped off the sheet, tore it up and threw the torn pieces into the wastebasket.

"What is it?" I asked. "Is it that bad?"

He said, "Reno police found where Amos Gage had been staying at an auto court. He'd registered under the name of Malcolm G. Beckley and had given the correct license number of his automobile, NFE 801. He paid his rent by the week. He left suddenly two days before the week was up. The manager of the motel has identified the picture of Amos Gage as the man who stayed there. There can't be any doubt about it."

"Well?" I asked. "The guy had to be somewhere."

"Don't you get it? He registered under the name of Beckley. But here's what's bad about it. One of the other tenants saw Gage with a shovel out in back of the building, digging a hole. She didn't think anything of it until after police started making inquiries, so they looked around and found the hole and dug and what do you think they found?"

"What did they find?" I asked.

"They found Malcolm Beckley's wrist watch, a five-hundred-dollar book of American Express checks with one fifty-dollar check torn out. They found a wallet with Beckley's driving license and all of his papers in it. They found his keys. They found his knife and they found a fountain pen with his name stamped on it in gold. They found a latent fingerprint on the back of the wrist watch. They processed that fingerprint and it's Gage's fingerprint."

I sat there and said nothing.

"There wasn't a cent of cash in the wallet," James went on.

I remained silent.

"Now then," James went on, "they've located the waitress who worked at the café run by Dorothy Lennox in Central Creek. She's the one who was on duty the night of the fifth. She remembers the occasion when Malcolm Beckley, Amos Gage and the blond hitchhiker came in and sat at a table and the blonde and Gage gulped down ham and eggs while Beckley put through a telephone call. She's identified Gage from a photograph and is being taken to Bakersfield to make a personal identification."

James sat and looked at me as though he had eaten something which made him very, very ill.

"That," I said, "looks rather bad as far as your side of the case is concerned."

After a moment James shook himself and said, "Well, of course, I can at least advance a theory."

"What theory?"

"That the blond hitchhiker was the one who committed the actual murder. She was the one who was in the back seat and she had the opportunity—in fact the only opportunity—to overpower the driver."

"Why did she do it?" I asked.

"Why does any hitchhiker kill the driver of the automobile? She wanted the automobile and she wanted the money."

"So after she killed him—you aren't going to claim she and Gage had hatched the crime up between them, are you?"

"Of course not. Then they'd be equally guilty and Amos would go to the gas chamber."

"I see," I said. "It was all the blonde's idea?"

"All her idea."

"Then after she had killed him, she turned around and gave all of the money to Gage. She gave him the guy's fountain pen. She gave him his wrist watch. She gave him his traveler's checks—now, why did she do that?"

James once more started rubbing the angle of his jaw. "The practice of criminal law, Donald," he said thoughtfully, "is one hell of a way to make a living. You can't give up. You've got to go in there fighting. You've got to see that the defendant has his day in court, that he has his rights in front of a jury. You have to remain enthusiastic about his case. You have to believe firmly in his innocence."

I nodded.

"And so," James said, "I have to stand up in front of a jury and let a district attorney make a goddam ass out of me."

"You aren't going to try to make a deal with him on pleading guilty?" I asked.

"Hell!" James said. "This district attorney wouldn't make a deal with me now on anything. He wouldn't agree to give the defendant five minutes of time or even a frosty smile if the defendant would plead guilty and ask the judge to sentence him to the gas chamber.

"In case you don't know it, Donald, the district attorney of this county is looking forward to standing up in front of a jury where he can prove every single element of a murder, step by step, piece by piece, and get a verdict of first-degree murder. What's more, he's going to get it before Amos Gage is thirty-five years of age, and half a dozen assorted charities are going to pat him on the back and tell him if they can ever do anything to further his political career they'll be only too glad to do it."

152

"What are *you* going to do?" I asked. "Are you going to quit?"

"Hell, no," he said. "I *can't* quit. If I quit now it would prejudice the defendant's case. I wish I'd been laid up in bed when the call came in to represent him. I wish I'd had small-pox or something, but I told him I'd represent him and I'm *going* to!"

There was nothing I could add and nothing he could subtract at that point, so I got up, shook hands and walked out.

14

I TOOLED THE AGENCY HEAP OVER THE Ridge Route, down into Los Angeles and drove to the office.

Bertha Cool was purring like a contented kitten. She beamed at me with a maternal air that was almost affectionate. "Donald, you little bastard," she said lovingly.

"What's the matter now?" I asked.

"You've done it again, haven't you?"

"Done what?"

Bertha picked up a couple of newspaper clippings. "The *Tribune*, Donald," she said. "My God, what a sheaf of publicity!"

I read what Malone had said about the agency.

"The sheriff of Kern County isn't going to be too enthusiastic about that," I said. "It makes it look as though all his office did was follow behind and pick up the pieces."

"Well, what the hell do we care about the sheriff of Kern County?" Bertha Cool demanded. "He doesn't pay us a thin dime! It's clients we want, Donald—customers, clients, persons who decorate the counter with the mazuma.

"And that reminds me, that perfectly delightful Mrs. Beckley was in. She's very practical-minded, Donald. She told me that of course she had to go through all the motions of being a bereaved widow, that actually she had been fairly happy with her husband but she realized that he wasn't the only man in the world . . . and then you know what, Donald?"

"What?"

"She asked about you."

"Where I was?"

"About *you,* you sly little devil! She wanted to know if you were married, if you were seriously interested in anyone, and then she paid her bill and the bonus and said she had another matter of employment but it was something she preferred to discuss with you personally because you were so familiar with the case—you're to go out there."

"What does she want?" I asked.

"Something about some sort of a follow-up, but she's loaded now, Donald—Damn you, don't you let her get her hooks into you! Don't you run out on Bertha and the partnership! She'll manufacture some excuse to take you to Europe with her as a bodyguard or something of that sort."

"Would you object to that?"

"Well . . . no, not as long as it's in the partnership, but don't you go running out and let her make you some individual proposition. If she wants to hire you as a member of the partnership, that's all to the good. Go to the South Pole with her if she wants."

The phone rang.

Bertha swept her glittering hand in an arc as she picked up the receiver, said, "Yes," then frowned and said, "Who wants him?"

I reached forward for the receiver. "I'll take my own calls if you don't mind, Bertha," I said.

She hung onto the phone for a minute, then almost threw it at me. "Go ahead," she said.

I said, "Hello. Donald Lam speaking."

Sandra Eden said, "This is Sandra, Mr. Lam. Mother wants to talk with you. Can you hold on just a minute?"

A moment later I heard Eleanore's voice on the phone. "Hello, Mr. Lam?"

"That's right."

"We're terribly, terribly concerned about Amos. Mr. Lam, isn't there something you can do?"

"On that, I don't know," I said.

"You know our financial circumstances. We hate to bother you but it does seem as though something should be done for poor Amos."

"I'll be in touch with you later on," I said, and hung up.

Bertha's eyes were pinpoints of hostility. "Damn it, Donald! That's that little mealy-mouthed whiney-face that was in here trying to get this outfit to locate some missing uncle who'd gone on a toot. What the hell are you doing, putting out time on charity stuff?

"I'll have you know this is a partnership. I'm entitled to have you work the way I work, and not go throwing away our services for nothing just because some spindle-shanked brat blinks back a few tears and looks up at you trustingly. She—"

She wanted someone to locate her Uncle Amos," I said.

"Uncle Amos, my foot!" Bertha snorted. "This is some guy that's been playing house with her mother, and the mother was ashamed to come in and ask what had happened to her meal ticket. Moreover, she didn't intend to spend a dime of her own money doing it.

"So she sent this little spindly legs along to try and hand us a line of malarkey and find out what had happened to Mother's meal ticket.

"If I thought you were dumb enough, sap enough and boob enough to fall for a line that—"

"She wanted to locate her Uncle Amos," I said. "Uncle Amos, do you get it, Bertha?"

Bertha blinked her eyes and said, "You mean this man

155

that murdered Malcolm Beckley was—Well, I'll be go-to-hell!"

Bertha lapsed into speechlessness.

"One and the same," I said.

"Fry me for an oyster!" Bertha muttered under her breath.

I waited for Bertha's brain to start functioning.

Suddenly Bertha shook her head as though something was making her dizzy and said, "Look, Donald, how the hell could that be? How could someone come in here and want us to find her husband, and a few minutes later somebody else wants us to look for Uncle Amos, who's missing, and it turns out that Uncle Amos murdered Malcolm Beckley and both cases came into this office within an hour of each other, and—Say, what the hell *is* this?"

"It's an interesting case," I said. "Have you got Daphne Beckley's number there?"

"Right here," Bertha said. "I had it all out for you on a memo."

I picked up the sheet of paper and told the operator to get me an outside line. I dialed Daphne Beckley's number.

After a moment Daphne's soft, seductive voice came over the line.

"This is Donald Lam," I said.

"Donald," she cooed. "I want you to come out here. I have something to discuss with you."

"I'm terribly tied up at the moment."

Bertha's diamond-studded hands made glittering motions indicating the door, indicating that I was to go on out.

"But, Donald," Daphne said, "can't you break away for just a little while?"

"Not right now. What seems to be the trouble?" I asked.

"Donald, have you seen the papers?"

"Not all of them."

"They published a picture of my husband's murderer."

"Well?"

"Donald, when I saw the picture I was startled. I thought it was my husband's picture. I thought they'd got the pictures mixed up."

"They look alike?" I asked.

"Look alike!" she exclaimed. "One of them could be the other one's twin brother. Now, that's what has to be done, Donald."

"What?" I asked.

She said, "I don't like to say this over the telephone. I don't like to say it at all. I don't like even to think it, but this could be the biggest hoax of all time."

"What do you mean? That you gave me the wrong picture and said it was you and your husband when in reality it was you and Amos?"

"Nothing like that! Don't think I'm *that* foolish."

"What then?"

"My husband may be trying to slip a fast one over on me. He may have pretended to be murdered and instead of that, he killed this hitchhiker and went off with the blonde. Everything he's done since could have been designed to throw everybody off the track—that business I heard on the radio about his having taken his traveler's checks, his driving license, and all of those things and buried them there at that auto court in Nevada . . . you don't hear about any cash money being buried there. He just got rid of the papers that he couldn't afford to have found on him."

"If he'd tried to frame a murder to fool the insurance company," I said, "he wouldn't have buried those things, he'd have left them on the body of the hitchhiker he killed. Moreover, they've taken fingerprints. The fingerprints are those of your husband."

"Well," she said slowly, "I suppose it's a fantastic theory. Now that I've listened to myself tell you about it, I know it sounds completely cockeyed, but—Donald, there's *something* wrong with this whole case."

"Such as what?"

"I don't know."

"Want to pay me to find out?" I asked.

157

"That was one of the things I had in mind. I . . . I want to be absolutely sure, Donald."

"How sure?" I asked.

"*Absolutely* sure. Donald, I wouldn't say this to anybody else but I'm going to tell you because you're so understanding. Malcolm was a sly one. It would be just like him to plan something like this so that he could keep an eye on me. There may be a detective shadowing me right now."

"Why would he want to have you shadowed?"

"Because he'd want to see what I did when I thought he was dead. In that way he might be able to get a divorce without giving me a dime. He'd want to see if I . . . if I . . . if I started running around with some man."

"Got one picked out?" I asked.

"Don't be conceited," she said archly.

"I don't get it," I told her.

"My, you can be dumb when you want to! For a man who is so brainy when he wants to be. . . . Why don't you come out here and talk things over with me?"

"I'm too busy."

"Too busy to let a client assign you to a problem?"

"Bertha Cool," I said, "makes all the business arrangements. After she makes the arrangements I go out on the cases. I guess you'll have to talk with Bertha. Call back in about ten minutes."

I hung up.

Bertha was beaming all over her face. "That's the way to talk to them, Donald," she said approvingly. "You let Bertha handle the business end, particularly with women.

"A woman can show you a little leg and you want to give the whole agency away. The only thing that interests me is the color of their money—Donald, do you suppose we can get in on some of this insurance money?"

"That," I told her, "is up to you."

"What was she talking about?"

"She thinks her husband is a sly one. She thinks he may have arranged some kind of a fake death."

158

"Wouldn't *that* be something!" Bertha said.

"But he didn't."

"Why?"

"Because," I said, "they got a good enough print from the fingers of the corpse to identify him. Fingerprints don't lie."

"Well, what gave her that idea in the first place?" Bertha asked.

"Because Amos Gage looks so much like her husband. She says the resemblance is startling."

"Could that be just a coincidence?" Bertha asked.

"There are lots of coincidences," I said. "It's a coincidence that Sandra Eden came in asking us to locate her Uncle Amos within a short time after Daphne Beckley had contacted you and asked us to find out what in the world had happened to her husband."

"You mean you've got an idea, don't you, Donald?"

"I have an idea," I said, "but it's cockeyed."

"Why is it cockeyed?"

"It has to be."

"Well, what is it?"

I said, "Suppose Malcolm Beckley was planning on taking a powder? Suppose he had met a very lovely blonde who had money and curves and intended to give him all he wanted of both?"

"Go on," Bertha said, her beady eyes glittering. "Don't stop now, Donald. The stuff that active brain of yours is digging up now is pure pay dirt. If there's any skulduggery in this case, Bertha will cash in on it. What happened?"

"Let's get back to Tom Allen," I said.

"Who's he?"

"The man who was on night shift at the Night & Day Garage at Rommelly."

"Okay. Go ahead."

I said, "We know he's a pushover for women."

Bertha nodded.

"And he has a criminal record," I said.

Again she nodded.

"All right," I told her. "Tom Allen meets a very sexy,

affable blonde. The blonde is on the make, and Tom Allen is on the make."

"Go on," Bertha said.

"Tom wants money and the blonde. The blonde wants money and Tom. Tom has just the right kind of a brain to think things up."

Bertha nodded.

"So," I said, "Tom knows that a blond hitchhiker can go down the road and stand at just the right place and someone is pretty certain to stop and offer her a lift. In fact, lots of people are going to."

Bertha nodded, silent with concentration.

"So," I said, "the blonde is rather choosy. She won't ride with a man and a woman, she won't ride in a cheap-looking car. She wants to ride in a car that looks like a million dollars. Along comes Malcolm Beckley in his Roadracer that's all souped up and loaded with accessories."

"Go ahead," Bertha said.

"That's for the blonde," I said. "She gets in the car. There are two men in the front seat. The blonde has a nice little leather shot-loaded billy concealed on her person."

"Hanging around her neck, down between her breasts," Bertha said, almost breathlessly. And then suddenly added, "Wait a minute, Donald. You're all wet. It was a jack handle."

"It was a jack handle that did the *killing,*" I said. "But I'm talking now about a slung shot or leather billy or sap."

"Go on, Donald," Bertha said, "you're doing the talking."

"At the right place in the road the blonde slips the sap out of her sweater and what does she do with it?"

"*What* does she do with it?" Bertha asked.

I said, "She couldn't hit the driver on the head first, because then the man who was seated next to him would grapple with her and there'd be a struggle. She might get the worst of it. But if she hits the passenger first, what's

160

the man driving the car going to do? He can't take both hands off the wheel without wrecking everybody, particularly on a mountain road. The most he can do is take one hand off the wheel."

Bertha nodded.

"So," I said, "she gives *him* a little love tap on the back of the head. Because it's a sap it doesn't crush his hat at all and it doesn't draw any blood."

"Then what?"

"Then," I said, "the blonde drives the car down the dirt road, stops it, gets out, takes the keys from the car, opens the trunk, gets out the jack handle and dumps out the driver. Then she drives the car another hundred yards and dumps out the other guy. Then she goes back with the jack handle and really finishes Malcolm Beckley. She makes a good job of that. She can't take any chances on his coming to. She needs a corpse that can be identified."

"Go on," Bertha said.

"But first," I said, "she takes everything out of Beckley's pockets, then she goes over to the other unconscious man and puts all of Beckley's stuff in his pockets, except perhaps a few hundred dollars which she holds out just on general principles because she hates to put money in the pockets of a sucker."

"And then?" Bertha asked breathlessly.

"Then," I said, "she hits the passenger a rather glancing blow with the jack handle, just enough to make a little blood—and then she's finished. She's all done for the day."

"What do you mean?" Bertha asked.

I said, "She goes over and sits down under a bush and waits for nature to take its course."

"In what way?"

"She waits for the passenger to wake up.

"Now, that's where luck played into her hands. It happened that when Gage woke up he didn't know where he was or what had been happening. But it wouldn't have made very much difference if he had known."

"What do you mean?"

161

"He woke up, regained consciousness. He's got a terrific headache, he's off the road. It's dark. The car is standing there with the door open and the motor running. What would you do?"

"You mean if I were the passenger?"

"That's right."

"I'd jump in the car and get the hell out of there before the blonde came back to finish me."

"Precisely," I said. "Then what would you do?"

"I'd drive like hell to the nearest town and then I'd call the police?"

"Exactly," I said. "And what would you tell the police?"

"I'd tell them about the blond hitchhiker and all of that, and I'd take them back to the place where I found the car."

"You're doing fine," I told her. "Keep on from there, Bertha."

"Then," Bertha said, "the police would look around with flashlights and they'd find—Now, wait a minute. Would they find the blonde?"

"Why should they?" I asked. "Why would the blonde wait around?"

"No, that's right," she said. "They'd find Beckley's body."

"That's good," I told her. "Then what would happen?"

"Then they'd search the pockets for identification and find that there wasn't any identification."

"And then?" I asked.

Bertha started blinking her eyes. "Why, fry me for an oyster!" she said. "They'd start asking the passenger questions. They'd want to know how he could prove that there *had* been a blonde, and—Why, damn it, Donald! The man couldn't prove there'd been a blonde. He couldn't prove anybody else had been in the automobile. He'd have all of Beckley's money and stuff in his pocket and he'd be identified as a down-and-out hitchhiker, and—Go on, Donald."

"And then what would happen?"

"Then he'd be indicted for murder and the cards would sure be stacked against him."

I nodded.

"But,"Bertha went on, "if that was the case . . . what did the blonde expect to gain? How could she make any money out of it—and why did she ring up Mrs. Beckley and tell her her husband had had a flat tire?"

"That," I said, "is the beauty of it. The blonde wasn't after the money Beckley had on him. She was after big-time stuff."

"Such as what?"

"Oh, probably about twenty grand," I said.

"What are you getting at, Donald?"

I said, "Remember the spendthrift trust. Amos Gage is going to come into a bunch of money when he reaches thirty-five if he hasn't been convicted of a major crime. If he has been convicted of a major crime, what happens to the money?"

"Charities," Bertha said.

"And if that provision in the will isn't absolutely iron-clad, if the trust can be knocked out, the trust funds would go to the legal heirs of Elbert Gage."

"Who are they?"

"For one thing, there's the widow of Amos Gage's brother."

"Who?"

"Sandra's mother, and Sandra herself, of course."

"What!" Bertha exclaimed.

"That's right," I said.

"But how could that trust be knocked out?"

"Apparently the will was executed within thirty days of the testator's death," I said. "In this state, if a will is executed within thirty days of the testator's death, only one-third of the estate can be left to charities. The rest has to be disposed of otherwise."

Bertha's eyes narrowed. Then they suddenly widened. "Donald, take a good, long second look at that little— Well, fry me for an oyster! How old is that brat?"

"Fifteen."

163

"Read what the FBI has to say about juveniles and crime," Bertha said. "These days the kids see lots of complicated detective shows on television. They get educated fast. . . . My God, Donald, it's the perfect crime! She could—Wait a minute! Wait a minute! Something's wrong here!"

"What's wrong?" I asked.

"That blond hitchhiker," Bertha said. "She wasn't supposed to enter the picture at all. She was supposed to be a story that Amos Gage told that no one would believe."

"If that's right," I said, "two things happened to change it."

"What were they?"

"The first was something no one could have anticipated. Beckley stopped at Central Creek to let the two hitchhikers gulp down ham and eggs. While they were doing that, he telephoned his wife and told her about the blond hitchhiker. That brought the blonde into the picture."

"Go on," Bertha said.

"Having been brought into the picture, she had to get out of the picture," I said. "Now, if Amos Gage had done what he was supposed to have done and had stopped at Rommelly and had yelled for the police and all of that, the blond hitchhiker would have faded out of the picture. But he didn't do that. He kept right on going. That put the conspirators in quite a fix. That could well account for the five-hour delay, why it was supposed to have taken five hours for Beckley to go the fifty miles between Central Creek and the place ten miles out of Rommelly where he was supposed to have broken down and had the flat tire."

"So the blonde had to go in and have a conference with Tom Allen?" Bertha asked.

"Could be," I said. "You're doing fine. Keep talking."

"And then Tom Allen told her to call Mrs. Beckley with this story about the flat tire."

I said nothing.

"That brings the blond hitchhiker into the picture," Bertha said, "but in view of the fact that Amos Gage had

164

made off with the car and the traveler's checks and all that, it took the blond hitchhiker right out of the picture."

"The story she told did," I said. "Remember, she said there'd been a flat tire and she had been elected as the one to go on and send a repair car back."

Bertha said, "You ran this Tom Allen guy on a lie detector?"

"We ran him on a lie detector," I said, "and the lie detector showed he was lying about not having had a call from a blonde on the morning of the sixth, so then the polygraph expert told him he was lying and then Tom Allen took a deep breath and confessed.

"That's where so many polygraph experts make a mistake. No one checked Tom Allen to see whether his confession was true or false."

"Donald," Bertha said, "I just can't believe it. And yet it's so damned logical that I can't disbelieve it."

"I told you," I said, "it's cockeyed. It's just an idea I'm playing around with."

"But what gave it to you in the first place?"

"It's so damned apropos," I said. "This business of Amos Gage getting just to the point where he was about to have a fortune in his hands and then suddenly getting involved in a murder case that is so dead open and shut you can't figure any way of squirming out of it. Then the fact that Mrs. Beckley comes in here to have us find out about her husband's disappearance and shortly after she comes in here Sandra Eden comes in."

"Why?" Bertha asked.

"It could be because she knew Daphne Beckley had been in and talked with you."

"And how would she know that?"

"There might be several answers to that," I said. "But remember that Sandra came in here right after Daphne Beckley had been in touch with you. Right afterward, remember. Not *before* but *after*—immediately after."

"Donald Lam," Bertha Cool said, "do you mean to stand there and tell me that little spindle-shanked brat has—By God, Donald, you're right! Why, that little strumpet, sitting there and blinking back the tears and being so brave and—Hell, she didn't give a damn whether we ever found Uncle Amos or not. All she wanted to do was to get Uncle Amos into the picture so that we'd cross his back trail while we were looking for Malcolm Beckley. . . . And, of course, they wanted to have a general alarm put out for Malcolm Beckley's car. They wanted to trace that Roadracer and . . . Amos Gage was bound to play into their hands, no matter *what* he did."

"That's right," I said. "The only thing they hadn't counted on was amnesia, but, as it happened, that worked out all right, too."

"Donald, what are you going to do about it?"

"Nothing," I said, "It's your theory. I just asked you questions. You were the one who furnished the answers."

Bertha glared at me. "You put the ideas into my mind. Now that you have, however, I can see the whole thing. . . . That two-faced little squirt!"

I said, "Better wait, Bertha."

"Wait for what?"

"Until you've met the trustee, Jerome L. Campbell. All I've been telling you is that someone decided to hang a murder rap around the neck of Amos Gage. This comes right at a time when some seven hundred and fifty thousand smackeroos are about to be turned over to someone. So we have to search for a motive."

"The trustee!" Bertha exclaimed. "What the hell has he—?"

She was interrupted by the telephone. Bertha picked it up, said, "Hello," then shoved the receiver at me. "It's for you."

"Who's calling?" I asked.

"Long distance," she said.

We have a switch in the office by which we can throw the telephone on to a loud-speaker and talk into a conference microphone.

Somehow I just had a hunch. I threw the switch and said, "Hello. This is Lam speaking."

The voice of Harvey Clover, the undersheriff, came

166

over the loud-speaker. "Lam," he said, "I hate to do this, but there's been a development in this Gage case."

"Shoot," I told him. "I'm interested in developments."

"You'll be interested in this one," he said.

"What is it?" I asked.

"Amos Gage has told the complete story of what happened. He's spilled everything."

"What did he say?" I asked.

"He says that you found him holed up in Reno, that you heard his story there and didn't communicate with the authorities, that you went down and found the body because you learned from him about where he had recovered consciousness.

"He says that you told him to sit tight there in Reno, not to waive extradition, to delay everything as much as possible until he passed thirty-five, that he intended to follow your advice but he got frightened, that because of what you told him he decided to get rid of all the Beckley property that he had. Then, having buried it there in Nevada, he decided he'd better get the hell out of Nevada, hoping that no one would ever trace him to Nevada."

"That's interesting," I said.

"That's a lot more than interesting," Clover said. "We don't like it, Lam. We don't like any part of it.

"It puts you in the position of being something of an accessory. It puts you in the position of working on inside information in order to go and find that corpse. It puts you in the position of concealing evidence in a murder case."

"And so what do you want?" I asked.

"We want you," Clover said.

"Coming to get me?" I asked.

"Sending for you," he said.

"How come?"

"I'm sticking my neck out on this," he told me. "I've persuaded the D.A. here not to take it to the Grand Jury until after he's had a chance to talk with you."

"Making anything public to the press?" I asked.

"Not yet."

"You want me over there?"

"We want you here. Now, the question is, do you come or do we send?"

"I'm coming," I told him and hung up.

Bertha Cool's eyes were glittering. "Donald," she said, "is there anything to that?"

"Anything to what?"

"About you getting in touch with Amos Gage?"

"Why not?" I said. "We were given a job finding him, remember?"

"What the hell do you mean, given a job?"

"Sandra Eden," I said, "wanted to find her Uncle Amos. Her mother, Eleanore, wanted to know where Amos was, but they didn't have any money to hire a detective agency and—"

"And you went around behind my back and walked right into that trap?"

"What do you mean, I walked right into a trap?" I said. "We gave ourselves an immunity bath."

"In what way?"

"We had two jobs," I said. "One of them was to locate Malcolm Beckley, the other one was to locate Amos Gage. I was protecting my client. I couldn't disclose Amos Gage's whereabouts until I had reported to my client. Of course, discovering a body was different. I had to report that to the authorities. But I didn't have to tell them all about how I knew where the body was."

"Our client!" Bertha screamed at me. "A skinny little brat that's been watching television and has planned a murder so she and her mother can get a bunch of money."

"Possibly," I said, "but you don't *know* that yet."

"The hell I don't!" Bertha said. "Your theory sold me."

"Well," I said, "perhaps if I can sell the district attorney of Kern County, we can make a deal."

I picked up my hat and walked out, leaving Bertha Cool sitting there speechless with anger and apprehension.

15

IT'S ABOUT TWO HOURS AND TWENTY-FIVE minutes fast driving time to Bakersfield.

I made it in just a little over two hours.

Harvey Clover looked at me with tight lips and stern eyes. "Lam," he said, "I stuck my neck out for you."

"Thanks."

"I tried to keep it out of the newspapers," he said, "but somehow there's been a leak. Did it come from your office?"

"Hell, no!" I said.

He handed me a paper damp from the press.

I looked at it. Headlines said, DETECTIVE IN DUTCH WITH D.A. There was the story that it was rumored Donald Lam, of the firm of Cool & Lam, who had been investigating the case, was to be interrogated by the district attorney, that the Grand Jury wanted very much to ask him certain questions.

The article went on to state that Lam had been unavailable but in a talk with his partner, Bertha Cool, it had been intimated that there would be "startling disclosures" when Lam went before the Grand Jury.

"What the hell!" I said.

"Your partner," Clover said, "what does she know about the case?"

"What I've told her."

"What else?"

"Nothing."

"All right," Clover said. "If you've got startling disclosures, you'd better get ready to make them. We're going in to see the D.A.."

The door opened and another deputy came in.

Clover made a surreptitious motion toward me and said, "I'll go see if the D.A. is ready."

"What kind of a guy is he?" I asked Clover.

"You'll find out," he said enigmatically.

He walked out.

I grinned at the deputy and said, "Well, you never can tell what a man'll do. How did it happen that Amos Gage told this story?"

The deputy simply shook his head and motioned to the newspaper. "That's all I know," he said.

I picked up the newspaper. There was a brief statement that Goodwin F. James had withdrawn as attorney for Amos Gage. That Amos Gage had then made a statement to the district attorney.

The article went on to state the case was to be rushed on for trial at the earliest possible date, that District Attorney Nunnely Ivan had promised there would be prompt action by the Grand Jury, and the case would be brought on for trial within a very short time, that the court calendar was in such shape that the case could be disposed of "promptly" and that the courts had agreed to cooperate in showing that justice in Kern County was swift.

There was an interview with Daphne Beckley. She posed for a photograph wearing dark glasses and showing a little leg. The district attorney said that the case against Amos Gage was so dead open and shut that he thought Gage would probably plead guilty, that if he didn't, the D.A.'s office had plenty of testimony to get a conviction of first-degree murder. Mrs. Beckley had been told she would be spared the harrowing experience of being forced to testify concerning the death of her husband. Mrs. Beckley, it stated, was at the moment prostrated with grief. Her doctor had recommended an ocean voyage.

Some sob sister had written up an interview with Mrs. Beckley. I was halfway through it when the door opened and Clover came back.

"This way, Lam," he said.

He took me down a corridor into an office marked *District Attorney—Enter,* pushed his way past several people who were in the office, shoved me through a door marked *District Attorney—Private*.

The door closed behind me, and Clover said, "Nunnely Ivan, Lam."

Nunnely Ivan was a big man of about forty-seven or eight, with intense black eyes set rather close together.

He didn't offer to shake hands. He said, "Sit down, Lam."

I sat down.

"I've heard a most disturbing story about you."

"What's disturbing about it?"

"You have apparently been an accessory after the fact."

"To what?"

"Murder."

"Whose murder?"

"Don't quibble," he said, raising his voice. "To the murder of Malcolm G. Beckley."

"In what way?" I asked.

"You counseled his murderer to keep out of the jurisdiction of the court, to conceal the evidence, and you didn't report the theft of Malcolm Beckley's car."

I yawned.

"Damn it!" Ivan said. "This is no light matter, Lam. You're going to lose your license, I can *promise* you that. And I think *maybe* you're going to lose your liberty. Now start yawning that one off."

I said, "I was protecting a client."

"No, you weren't," Ivan said. "I've talked with Mrs. Beckley on the telephone. You didn't have any instructions from her to cover up on anything. She wanted her husband found. She—"

"I'm not talking about Mrs. Beckley," I said. "I'm talking about relatives of Amos Gage."

He blinked his eyes at that one. "What relatives?"

I said, "A fifteen-year-old girl who was trying her best to be brave but who felt that something terrible had happened to her Uncle Amos."

That was a new angle. Ivan became thoughtful.

"Now then," I said, "I see by the paper that Mrs.

171

Beckley is to be spared the ordeal of appearing before the Grand Jury and in court."

"That's neither here nor there," he said curtly. "We're talking about you now, not about Mrs. Beckley."

"That's fair enough," I said. "Mind if I use the phone?"

"What do you want?" he asked.

"In the first place," I said, "what's Mrs. Beckley's number? Never mind, I have it here."

I took out my notebook, picked up the telephone, turned to the district attorney and said, "Whose suggestion was it that she didn't need to testify? Yours or hers?"

"Mine," he said. "I told her she could be spared the ordeal and all of the publicity."

I said into the telephone, "I want to talk with the long-distance operator who handles calls from Central Creek and also from Rommelly. I suppose they go through some central exchange?"

"That's right," the operator said. "Is this the district attorney's office?"

"Yes, it is," I told her.

"Who's talking?" she asked.

"Lam," I said. "Get the call through right away, will you?"

After a moment a voice said, "Yes, what is it, please?"

I said, "I'm trying to check some long-distance calls on the night of the fifth and the morning of the sixth. First I want to check a call from Carver City to Edgemont 6-5589. Then I want to check a call from Central Creek about thirty-five minutes later to Edgemont 6-5589, and then I want to check a call from Rommelly about five o'clock in the morning to Edgemont 6-5589."

"What the hell are you doing?" Ivan demanded irritably.

"Doing something you should have thought of a little earlier," I said. "Just checking those long-distance calls."

"There's no need to check them," Ivan said. "I have Mrs. Beckley's sworn statement on those calls. She's given me the time and the conversation. In the two calls that she had from her husband she says she recognized

172

his voice and can swear that it was her husband talking. That enables me to prove the calls if I have to."

"That's nice," I said.

"Hang up the phone," Ivan said suddenly. "I think this is some kind of a stall. We'll do our own investigative work."

I said, "You mean you haven't checked those calls?"

"Of course we haven't checked them. We've got the testimony of the woman who received them. The—"

Harvey Clover said, "Wait a minute, Nunnely. This is just mopping up but let's just check and get the times verified."

I hung on for a minute, then the operator's voice said, "We have no call from Carver City, no call from Central Creek, no call from Rommelly to Edgemont 6-5589."

I said, "If someone had put through a long-distance call and there had been no answer, what would have happened?"

"The ticket would have been destroyed if the call was canceled and no one talked on it," she said.

"I think you'd better tell that to the district attorney," I said. "Just a moment."

I turned to Ivan and said, "There are no tickets on calls from Carver City, from Central Creek or from Rommelly on the fifth or the sixth. If calls had been placed but there had been no answer and the calls canceled, the tickets would have been destroyed and there would have been no record. If there had been conversations on the calls then there would have been a record—you want to talk with the long-distance operator?"

Ivan grabbed the phone out of my hands.

"This is the district attorney, Nunnely Ivan," he said. "Now look, we know those calls went through and we know about what time. I want them traced."

He screwed his face all up in an expression of extreme irritation and shouted into the phone, "Damn it! I tell you those calls went through! I have the sworn statement of the party at the other end."

He lapsed into frowning silence, then said, "Now look,

173

we can't slip up on this thing. I've got to know. Those calls were made. Now, there's something wrong with your bookkeeping. Get busy."

Ivan slammed up the telephone, turned to me. "I've had enough of your insolence, Lam. I've tried to protect you. Now I've done all I'm going to."

He nodded to Clover, picked up a receiver and said, "All right. Send in the reporters."

The corridor echoed to feet. The door opened.

I settled back in my chair and lit a cigarette.

"Gentlemen," Nunnely Ivan said, "I've tried to keep this thing under cover as much as possible because I didn't want to be a party to an injustice. This is Donald Lam. He is a private detective from Los Angeles. He has become involved in this case and he had been named by Amos Gage in a statement which Gage made in my office earlier today."

A photographer blinded me with a flashbulb. One of the reporters pulled out a bunch of folded newsprint and said to Ivan, "Would you care to make a statement, Mr. District Attorney?"

Ivan hesitated.

My friend, Frank Malone, looked at me and frowned. "*You* got anything to say, Lam?" he asked.

"Lots," I said. "I'm going to give an interview to the press."

"Go ahead," Malone said.

I said, "The district attorney has just made a startling discovery. There is no record whatever of any calls from Carver City, Central Creek or Rommelly to the residence of Malcolm G. Beckley. Daphne Beckley, the widow, states that she received three calls—one from her husband at Carver City, one about thirty-five minutes later from Central Creek and one five hours later from a blond hitchhiker at Rommelly. The district attorney has ascertained that there is no record of any of those calls, that if those calls had been put through there would have been a record, that the only reason there is no record is that there was no answer and the calls were canceled.

174

"This means," I said, "that Daphne Beckley is lying when she says she received the calls. It also means that she wasn't home on the night of the fifth and the sixth.

"Thanks to Harvey Clover here, the police are now working on a red-hot theory. In short," I said, "the blond hitchhiker who actually existed was none other than Daphne Beckley, wearing a blond wig, using tinted contact lenses to change the color of her eyes, and working by prearrangement with her husband in a well thought out scheme by which they were to collect a hundred and fifty thousand dollars' insurance."

"Hey, wait!" Ivan shouted. "You can't—"

Harvey Clover was blinking his eyes at me. He held up a hand, palm outward, toward Ivan and said, "Wait a minute, Nunnely, wait a minute. He's talking. Let him talk."

I said, "Malcolm Beckley was making lots of money but was broke. He had insurance of a hundred and fifty thousand dollars in case of death by violence. He and his wife planned a perfect crime.

"It all started when they stumbled on a man who had a startling resemblance to Malcolm Beckley. His name was Amos Gage. They studied Gage's habits. They made a surreptitious appraisal of his contacts, the friends who would be apt to miss him if he disappeared. If we take the time and trouble, we'll probably find that a detective agency was employed to furnish a complete background on Amos. They learned that he was a periodic drunkard. They followed Gage on his last drunk. When he got to a service station and wanted to hitchhike home, Malcolm Beckley came along very fortuitously—actually, all this was part of a plan.

"He picked up Gage, put him in the front seat.

"They started out of Carver City. A few miles out of Carver City they met the mysterious blond hitchhiker who actually was Daphne Beckley, Malcolm Beckley's wife, wearing a blond wig, contact lenses and dressed to show

175

all of her curves, some of which may have been accentuated slightly with artificial lures, so to speak.

"She got in the back seat.

"Beckley stopped at Central Creek ostensibly to feed his hitchhikers. His actual purpose was to lay the foundation for a telephone call which Mrs. Beckley could state she received and which would give her an alibi.

"Beckley went over to the phone, pretended to carry on a conversation but was actually talking into a dead line. He came back and picked up his hitchhikers. After they had driven along the road toward Rommelly to a prearranged spot, Mrs. Beckley smacked down on Amos Gage's head with a slung shot. Then they took Gage off the highway, down a dirt road and there they got out the jack handle. They intended to beat his face to a pulp. They also intended to leave him until his body would be badly decomposed by the time it was discovered. They took all of the things out of Malcolm Beckley's pocket and put them in Gage's pockets so that the body would be identified as that of Malcolm Beckley.

"Then is when Malcolm chickened out. Right at the last he couldn't take it. His stomach rebelled and he upchucked. He probably went down to the creek to wash. It was then his wife fully realized her position for the first time. She had engaged in a murder conspiracy with a guy who didn't have the nerve to go through with it. If she killed Amos, she knew Malcolm would weaken in case he was ever questioned and would babble out a confession that would send them both to the gas chamber.

"So why risk her life to provide a substitute corpse? All she needed was a dead husband to become a wealthy widow. Why not kill both men and let the mysterious woman hitchhiker take the blame? She had an alibi given to her by her husband himself.

"It was a swell idea and it flashed into her mind and she put it into almost instant execution. Then, before she could get back and transfer the things out of Amos' pockets to her husband's clothes, Amos returned to consciousness. He climbed in the car and drove away.

176

"The perfect crime had gone slightly askew, but the slip-up wasn't really important. Mrs. Beckley had her corpse which was worth a hundred and fifty thousand smackers to her. She could now blame the crime on Amos. So she walked to Rommelly, went to a garage and ordered a repair car sent back.

"When she went in there, her idea was that the repair car would go back and find nothing on the road, but the young man who was in charge of the garage at the time looked pretty good to her. She saw an opportunity to really impress him and so they sat there and talked about things other than sending a repair car back. By the time Mrs. Beckley was ready to leave, Tom Allen didn't see any use in sending a repair car at all."

Nunnely Ivan started to say something, then checked himself.

"The sheriff's office," I said, "through some clever detective work by Harvey Clover, has located Tom Allen's shaving mirror, which was used by the mysterious blond hitchhiker. It contains one perfect latent fingerprint and a couple of smudges. The latent fingerprint is being traced. There is every reason to believe it will match the print of the right-hand little finger of Daphne Beckley."

I sat back and lit a cigarette.

"Now look," Frank Malone said, "we want a confirmation of this from—"

Clover jumped to his feet. "Gentlemen," he said, "we had no idea that Donald Lam was going to say so much. He has been co-operating with the office, but we were not prepared to make some of these announcements as yet. We're going to ask you to hold off for a few minutes."

"Hold off something like this?" Malone asked. "You're crazy."

Clover turned on him. "Get out," he said. "This has gone too far. Damn it, Lam! You had no business letting the cat out of the bag!"

"I thought you wanted me to make a statement to the press," I said. "Wasn't that why you called them in?"

177

"Not that," he said. "Get out of here now, all of you. We'll have a formal statement within . . ." He looked at Ivan. "Within half an hour, Nunnely?"

"Make it forty minutes, Harvey," Ivan said.

16

BERTHA COOL READ THE PAPERS AND looked at me. "You little sonofabitch," she said.

I said nothing.

"How in hell did you know, Donald?"

I said, "Daphne Beckley was taking it too hard all of a sudden. Her doctor advised her to take an ocean trip, and the district attorney told her she didn't need to testify. I started putting two and two together—I couldn't understand the coincidences in the case until I started thinking them out carefully.

"I think I overlooked the most important clue in the whole business, which was that Sandra Eden said she went to a librarian friend and asked her for some good detective agency. The librarian referred her to us. If the Beckleys had detectives checking on Sandra, it's a cinch they learned about the librarian and her advice. So Mrs. Beckley worked it so we were drawn into the play. That couldn't have been sheer coincidence. It means the Beckley woman was checking on Sandra. Beckley's body had been too long undiscovered. His widow was getting nervous."

"Fry me for an oyster!" Bertha said. "And you let the cat out of the bag over there in Bakersfield, and Daphne scribbled a confession and then took a half a bottle of sleeping pills."

"That's easier than the gas chamber," I said. "Or sitting in a woman's penitentiary watching your youth slip through your fingers."

Bertha picked up the check on the desk in front of her.

"The insurance company would have been stuck for a hundred and fifty grand," she said. "They have an association that provides rewards for detecting insurance frauds. Here is a check for ten grand from that association—think of it—ten thousand smackeroos."

"Chicken feed," I said. "Think of Amos Gage reaching thirty-five and inheriting seven hundred and fifty thousand dollars."

Bertha heaved a deep sigh. "Sometimes," she said, "I think you're the most exasperating bastard in the world, and other times I just choke up thinking of the mental acrobatics you—

"You're like a trapeze performer, whirling around so damned fast nobody can be sure just what you're doing and taking such chances you scare the daylights out of me."

I motioned toward the check from the insurance company.

"The money doesn't scare you, does it?"

Bertha heaved a big sigh. "*You* scare me. Donald, I'm going to be frank with you. If I weren't so goddam avaricious I'd dissolve this partnership while I still had my liberty."

"But you're not going to do it?"

"Hell, no. Go out and get hold of this Amos Gage and cut us in on some more of that gravy. If Bertha is going to gamble, she may as well shoot the works!"